'Miss Read', or in real life Mrs Dora Saint, is a teacher by profession who started writing after the Second World War, beginning with light essays written under her own name mainly for *Punch*. She has written on educational and country matters for various journals, and worked as a script-writer for the B.B.C.

'Miss Read' is married, with one daughter, and lives in a tiny Berkshire hamlet. Her hobbies are theatre-going, listening to music and reading. She is a local magistrate and, of course, a manager of the local village school!

'Miss Read' has published numerous books, including *Village School* (1955), *Village Diary* (1957), *Thrush Green* (1959), *Fresh from the Country* (1960), *Winter in Thrush Green* (1961), *Miss Clare Remembers* (1962), an anthology, *Country Bunch* (1963), *Over the Gate* (1964), *The Market Square* (1966), *Village Christmas* (1966), *The Howards of Caxley* (1967), *Fairacre Festival* (1968), *News from Thrush Green* (1970), two books for children, *Hobby Horse Cottage* and *Hob and the Horse-bat*, and The Red Bus Series for the very young. Her most recent books are *Farther Afield* (1974), *No Holly For Miss Quinn* (1976) and *Village Affairs* (1977).

Many of 'Miss Read's' books are published in Penguins.

'MISS READ'

Battles at Thrush Green

PENGUIN BOOKS

Penguin Books Ltd, Harmondsworth, Middlesex, England
Penguin Books, 625 Madison Avenue, New York, New York 10022, U.S.A.
Penguin Books Australia Ltd, Ringwood, Victoria, Australia
Penguin Books Canada Ltd, 2801 John Street, Markham, Ontario, Canada L3R 1B4
Penguin Books (N.Z.) Ltd, 182–190 Wairau Road, Auckland 10, New Zealand

—

First published by Michael Joseph Ltd 1975
Published in Penguin Books 1978
Reprinted 1979

—

Copyright © Miss Read, 1975
All rights reserved

—

Set, printed and bound in Great Britain by
Cox & Wyman Ltd, London, Reading and Fakenham
Set in Monotype Bembo

To Norah
For Times Remembered
With Love

Contents

PART ONE

Alarms and Excursions

1. Albert Piggott is Overworked

At a quarter to eight one fine September morning, Harold Shoosmith leant from his bedroom window and surveyed the shining face of Thrush Green.

The rising sun threw grotesquely elongated shadows across the grass. The statue of Nathaniel Patten cast one a dozen times its own length, with the head and shoulders at right angles to the rest, where it was thrown against the white palings next door to 'The Two Pheasants'.

The shabby iron railings round the churchyard made cross-hatchings on the green, and the avenue of chestnut trees, directly in front of Harold's window, formed a shady tunnel with a striped floor of sunshine and shadow.

The view filled Harold Shoosmith with deep contentment. This was the place for retirement! After years in Africa, moving from one post to another, each hotter and more humid than the last, he had come home to roost at Thrush Green, the birthplace of Nathaniel Patten, whose missionary work he had so much admired, and whose memorial he had been instrumental in establishing.

But no living figures were apparent on this bright morning, with the exception of the Youngs' old spaniel Flo, who was ambling about examining the trees in the avenue in a perfunctory fashion. Nevertheless, the sound of distant whistling alerted Harold.

Someone in the wings was about to enter the empty stage, and very soon the stout figure of Willie Bond, one of Thrush Green's postmen, emerged from the lane, which leads to Nod and Nidden, and propped his bicycle against the hedge.

Tightening the belt of his dressing-gown, Harold Shoo-smith descended the stairs to greet his first caller.

'You gotter mushroom as big as a nouse in your 'edge,' announced Willie, handing in half a dozen letters.

'Let's see,' said Harold, following him down the path. Sure enough, at the foot of his hawthorn hedge, stood a splendid specimen, as big as a saucer, but young and beautiful. Two or three fine pieces of grass criss-crossed its satin tip where it had pushed its way into the world and, underneath, the gills were rosy pink and unbroken.

'Do fine for your breakfast,' said Willie, putting one foot on the pedal of his bicycle.

'Too much for me,' said Harold. 'Why don't you take it? After all, you found it.'

Willie shook his head.

'Never touches 'em. Them old things are funny. My auntie, down the mill, she died after havin' a dish of them for breakfast.'

'Surely she must have eaten toadstools by mistake?'

'Maybe. But she died anyway.'

He mounted his machine and began to weave away.

'Mind you,' he called back, 'she'd had dropsy for five years, but we always reckon it was the mushrooms what done for her in the end.'

Harold bent and retrieved the mushroom. The fragrance, as it left the ground, made him wonder, for one brief moment, if he could bother to cook some of it with a couple of rashers for his breakfast, as Willie had advised.

But he decided against it and, returning to the kitchen, set about making his usual coffee-and-toast repast, using the upturned mushroom as decoration for the breakfast table.

His morning mail was unremarkable. Two bills, one receipt, a bulky and unsolicited package from *Reader's*

Digest which must have cost a pretty penny to produce and was destined for the wastepaper basket unread, and a post-card from his old friend and neighbour Frank Hurst and his wife Phil, posted in Italy two weeks before, and extolling the beauties of the scenery.

It was while he was sipping his second cup of coffee, and wondering idly why literary men always seemed to write such a vile hand, that the door burst open to reveal Betty Bell, his exuberant domestic help. As always, she was breath-less and smiling. She might just have galloped up the steep hill from Lulling non-stop, but in fact, as Harold well knew, she had simply wheeled her bicycle from the village school next door where she had been 'putting things to rights' for the past half-hour.

'How's tricks then?' inquired Betty, struggling out of her coat. 'All fine and dandy? Wantcher study done first or the bed? Laundry comes today, you know.'

Harold did his best to look alert and to switch to the faster tempo of activity which Betty's arrival always occasioned.

'Study, I think. I've still to dress and shave. I'm rather behind this morning.'

'Well, time's your own, now you're retired.'

Her eye lit upon the mushroom.

'What a whopper! Where'd you find that?'

'Willie Bond found it. It was growing just the other side of the hedge. Would you like it?'

Betty Bell gave a shudder.

'I wouldn't touch it if it was the last thing on earth to eat. Not safe, them things. Why, my old auntie died of eating mushrooms. Honest, she did!'

Betty's eyes grew round with awe.

'What an extraordinary thing,' exclaimed Harold. 'So did Willie's aunt!'

'Nothing extraordinary about it,' replied Betty, rummaging in the dresser drawer for a clean duster. 'She was my auntie too. Me and Willie Bond's cousins.'

She swept from the room like a mighty rushing wind, leaving Harold to ponder on the ever-enthralling complications of village life.

Some time later, Harold emerged from his front door bearing the mushroom in a paper bag. Behind him the house throbbed with the sound of the vacuum cleaner and Betty Bell's robust contralto uplifted in song.

It was good to be away from the noise. The air was fresh. A light breeze shook a shower of lemon-coloured leaves from the lime trees, and ruffled Harold's silver hair, as he set off across the grass to the rectory. He had remembered that the Reverend Charles Henstock and his wife Dimity were both fond of mushrooms.

On his way he encountered the sexton of St Andrew's. The church stood at the south-western corner of Thrush Green, and Albert Piggott's house was placed exactly opposite it and next door to 'The Two Pheasants'. Albert divided his time, unequally, between the two buildings.

The sunshine and serenity of the morning were not reflected in Albert's gloomy face. Hands in pockets, he was mooching about among the tombstones, kicking at a tussock of grass now and again and muttering to himself.

'Good morning, Piggott,' called Harold.

'A good morning for some, maybe,' said Albert sourly, approaching the railings. 'But not for them as 'as this sort of mess to clear up.'

Harold leant over the railings and surveyed the graveyard. Certainly there were a few pieces of paper about, but to his eye it all looked much as usual.

'I suppose people throw down cigarette boxes and so on when they come out of the pub,' he remarked, 'and they blow over here. Too bad when there's a litter box provided.'

'It's not the paper as worries me,' replied Albert. 'It's this 'ere grass. Since my operation, I can't do what I used to do.'

'No, no. Of course not,' said Harold, assuming an expression of extreme gravity in deference to Albert's operation. Thrush Green was learning to live with Albert Piggott's traumatic experience, as related by him daily, but was finding it a trifle exhausting.

'Take a look at it,' urged Albert. 'Take a proper look! What chance is there of pushin' a mower up these 'ere paths with the graves all going which-way? One time I used to scythe it, but Doctor Lovell said that was out of the question. "Out of the question, Piggott," he said to me, same as I'm saying to you now. "Out of the question." His very words.'

'Quite,' said Harold.

'And take these railings,' went on Albert, warming to his theme. 'When was they put up, eh? You tell me that. When was they put 'ere?'

'A good while ago,' hazarded Harold.

'For Queen Victoria's Golden Jubilee, that's when,' said Albert triumphantly. 'Not 'er Diamond one, but 'er *Golden* one! That takes you back a bit, don't it? Won't be long afore these railings is a 'undred years old. Stands to reason they're rusted. 'Alf of 'em busted, and the other 'alf ought to be pulled out. There was always this nice little stub wall of dry stone. That don't wear too bad, but these 'ere railings 'as 'ad it!'

Harold looked, with more attention, at Albert Piggott's territory. To be sure, he had some grounds for grumbling. Tall rank weeds grew inside the stub wall, nettles, the rusty spires of docks, cow-parsley with skeleton umbels turning papery as the summer waned, with convolvulus entwining all and thrusting its tentacles along the railings.

The tombstones stood among hillocks of grass which had

grown beyond a mower's powers, as Albert had said. Here and there, a few grassy mounds, neatly shorn, paid tribute to the loving hands of relatives who did their best to honour the resting places of their dead. But these islands of tidiness only served to throw the neglected whole into sharp contrast.

Albert was right about the railings too, Harold observed. Several had splintered with rust and would be dangerous to handle.

'Is there any need for the railings, I wonder?' said Harold, musing aloud.

'There's need all right,' responded Albert. 'That's why they was set 'ere. In the old days there used to be cows and that, grazing on the green, and they could get over this liddle ol' wall easy as kiss your 'and. And the kids too. You gotter keep people and animals out of a churchyard, stands to reason.'

'You won't keep people out for ever,' pointed out Harold, preparing to go on his way. 'We'll all be in there together before long.'

'Some sooner than others,' retorted Albert, with a morose sniff, as Harold departed.

The rectory, some hundred yards from St Andrew's, was a high Victorian monstrosity, facing north, and perched on a small mound the better to catch the chilly winds of the Cotswold country.

It was, thought Harold, as he waited on the doorstep, the most gloomy house in Thrush Green. Unlike its neighbours, which were built of local stone, the rectory had been encased in grey stucco early in its life. The ravages of time had caused pieces to break away here and there, so that newer patches of different grey made the whole affair appear shabbier than ever.

Large sash windows and a tall narrow front door were all

in need of paint, but there was little money to spare, as Harold knew too well. In any case, Charles Henstock cared little for creature comforts, and had lived for several years alone, in appalling conditions of cold and discomfort, until his marriage to Dimity Dean a few years before had brought companionship and a slight mitigation of the hardship of his surroundings.

Dimity opened the door to him and greeted him with cries of welcome.

'What a day you've brought with you! I'm in the kitchen, and the sun is just streaming in.'

She led the way, still chattering, down the long dark corridor which acted as a wind tunnel, and kept the rectory in a state of refrigeration during the winter months. Harold's feet echoed on the shabby linoleum, and he thought guiltily of his own carpeted home across the green. It was shameful to think how appallingly some of the clergy were housed. Charles's stipend was barely enough to keep body and soul together, as Harold well knew. Not that he or Dimity ever complained. Their hearts were thankful, their concern for others governed all their thoughts. They were two of the happiest people Harold had ever met. But he grieved for their poverty secretly, whilst marvelling at their shining goodness.

The kitchen was certainly the most cheerful place in the house. It was the only downstairs room which faced south, and the comfortable smell of cooking added to the warmth of its welcome after the bleakness of the rest of the house.

'Charles is writing letters in the study,' said Dimity. 'I'll let him know that you're here. Do find a seat.'

'Don't bother him,' said Harold, but she had gone already, fluttering up the dark passage, still uttering little cries of pleasure at his visit.

Harold sat down by the kitchen table, first removing a pile

of parish magazines from the seat. He observed Dimity's cooking paraphernalia with interest.

A pudding basin stood close to him, and a piece of pastry was in the process of being rolled out. A floury rolling pin lay dangerously near the table's edge, and Harold moved it prudently to a more central position. Something was sizzling gently in a frying pan, and Harold hoped that Dimity would return before it needed attention. His own culinary skills were enough for self-preservation, but he did not feel equal to attending to other people's creations.

A large tabby cat was curled up on the sunny window sill. Harold had known it since it was a kitten. It was one of a litter born to Dotty Harmer's cat, and it was sheer luck that Harold did not own a cat himself from that household. The eccentric Miss Harmer, animal-lover and amateur herbalist, was a power to be reckoned with when she had a litter of kittens needing homes. The Henstocks' cat, Tabitha, seemed to have struck lucky, thought Harold, looking at the array of saucers set down for it by the sink.

Dimity and Charles entered.

'I'm sorry to have interrupted the letter writing,' said Harold.

Charles Henstock's plump face was creased with a smile.

'I can always set aside letter writing,' he assured his friend. 'It's a task I abhor, especially when there are a score of complaints to answer.'

'Such as?'

'Why is the church so cold? Why didn't I see the kneeler that mother gave in 1892, when I visited the church recently? Why is Uncle Thomas's grave so neglected?'

'Poor Charles!' murmured Dimity. 'It's really too bad of people to worry him so.'

She turned her attention to the piece of dough.

'Do you mind if I finish this? It's going to be a steak and

kidney pudding, and it should have been on an hour ago.'

'I'm not going to stop,' said Harold, rising. 'But I thought you might like this.'

He handed over the paper bag.

'It couldn't have come at a better time,' cried Dimity. 'I shall put half in the pudding and keep the other half to fry with the breakfast bacon tomorrow morning.'

'Don't go yet,' said Charles. 'Come into the study, out of Dimity's way, and perhaps she would make us some coffee when the pudding's in.'

'Of course, of course,' she exclaimed, her eyes still on the massive mushroom. 'I'll call you the minute it's ready.'

Reluctantly, Harold followed his friend to the study. It was a lofty room, with dark green walls and an inadequate strip of thin carpeting lying in front of the great desk which dominated the room. A crucifix hung on the wall behind the rector's head, flanked by several fading photographs from college days.

From his chair, Harold could see, through the window, the thatched cottage across the way where Dimity had lived before her marriage. She had shared it with Ella Bembridge, another of Thrush Green's redoubtable spinsters, who still lived there, coming over to see her old friend at least once a day.

If anything, Harold was rather more afraid of the ruthless Ella than he was of scatter-brained Dotty Harmer. The latter he could dodge. Ella never gave up. How Dimity could have survived such a partnership for so many years, he just did not know. Another instance of her selflessness, he supposed, although he was ready to admit that Ella's gruffness no doubt hid a warm heart. At least, that's what people told him at Thrush Green, and he was only too willing to believe them.

Certainly, her cottage, glimpsed through the rectory window, looked as snug as a cat sunning itself. Its thatch gleamed. A row of hollyhocks swayed in the breeze, and Ella's open bedroom window flashed dazzling lights as it reflected the sunshine. Did Dimity ever regret leaving that haven, he wondered?

He looked at Charles, turning the papers on his desk. It had been no sacrifice for Dimity, Harold decided, when she gave up her home across the road. There was no finer man than the rector of Thrush Green.

'Do you get many letters of complaint?' he asked.

'A few each week. I try and keep one morning a week for answering them. I don't quite know what I am expected to do. Some are most unreasonable – this kneeler one, for instance. But of course people are distressed and I must do my best to explain things, and perhaps to comfort them.'

'We might do something about the churchyard between us,' said Harold diffidently. 'I saw Piggott as I came across, and of course he's past keeping the place as it should be.'

'I've done my utmost to get another man,' replied Charles, 'but no one seems to want the work.'

'We might organize a working party,' suggested Harold. 'We could take down the railings, for instance. They're getting downright dangerous.'

'They are in a bad way,' agreed the rector, 'but I think we should probably have to get a faculty to remove them. I must go into it.'

A cry from the kitchen told them that coffee was ready.

'Of course,' went on the rector, following his friend down the passage, 'Piggott never makes the best of anything. No one could accuse him of looking on the bright side of life. However, I will go and see what can be done during the week. Thrush Green must have a tidy churchyard.'

'Yes indeed,' echoed Dimity, passing steaming cups. 'Thrush Green must have a tidy churchyard.'

Had they known it, on that serene September morning, those simple words were to become a battle cry. The resting place of Thrush Green's dead was soon to become a field of conflict.

2. Miss Fogerty is Upset

Thrush Green, which is roughly triangular, is bordered by two highways which converge at the southern end in Lulling. A fine avenue of chestnut trees lines the third side at the northern end, joining the two roads.

Harold Shoosmith's house stands on the smaller road which leads northward to the villages of Nod and Nidden. Next door stands the village school, one or two cottages, including Albert Piggott's, and 'The Two Pheasants'.

The other road is larger and busier, leading northward to other Cotswold towns, and finally to the Midlands. It is on this road, facing across the green to the village school and public house, that some of Thrush Green's most attractive houses stand, although the finest of all, everyone agrees, are the three magnificent dwellings whose frontages lie along the chestnut avenue.

Ella Bembridge's cottage, at the head of the steep hill which drops down to Lulling High Street, is one of the pretty houses on the main road and Dr and Mrs Bailey live in another, a solid Cotswold stone house weathered to a perfect blend of grey and gold.

Next door to the Baileys' stands a small square house, of the same age, called Tullivers, and to this house, some time ago, came a young woman and her little son Jeremy. Thrush Green, of course, was avidly interested in the newcomer and speculated about the non-appearance of her husband.

But speculation turned to sympathy when Thrush Green heard that he had been killed in a car crash in France, and sympathy turned to rejoicing when she married again later. Frank and Phyllida Hurst were popular members of the

Thrush Green community, and young Jeremy one of the star pupils at the village school.

On this sparkling September morning, as the rector, his wife and their visitor sipped their coffee, Phil Hurst was cutting roses in the garden of Tullivers. This second flowering was infinitely better than the first, she decided, snipping busily. Just as second thoughts usually were – or second marriages, perhaps?

She straightened up and stood, silent, lost in her thoughts. Across the green the schoolchildren shouted in the playground. From a garden nearby came the sound of a lawn mower, and swallows, strung along the telegraph wire like beads on a thread, chattered together. But Phil heard nothing.

The old tag: 'Comparisons are odious' came into her mind. It was true in this case. This second marriage was wonderfully, strongly happy despite the difference in their ages. But no one could say that it was better than the first – simply different. Marriage with John had been a gay affair, exciting and exacting, two young people learning to live together – until the last unhappy months when he had left her for a French woman.

Marriage with Frank was happiness in a different way. It had a quieter, more companionable quality. It was Frank who gave comfort, whereas it was she who had comforted John. There was a solid strength about the older man which John had lacked, but which she had never realized until now.

And then he was so good with Jeremy! How heartwarming that was, to see the affection between them! It would have been understandable if a man of Frank's age had shown some irritation now and again in the presence of a vociferous little boy. After all, Robert, his only son by his first marriage, who was now a farmer in Wales, had four children of his own, and Frank's youngest grandchild was much the same age as Jeremy.

She moved thoughtfully towards the house where a Golden Shower rose flaunted its lemon flowers against the stone wall. At the moment there was one flaw in their otherwise perfect relationship. Frank dearly wanted Jeremy to go away to school, positive that it brought out the best in any child. Phil hated the idea, at least until he was considerably older. He loved his present school. He loved Tullivers and the simple life of Thrush Green. He had lost his father, and had had to adapt to another man taking his father's place. Phil felt sure that it was best to let him stay as he was for some time.

There was a good day school in Lulling which Paul Young attended, and he was going on from there to his father's public school. Phil thought that this was the ideal plan, and decided that she must speak to her friend Joan Young, who lived in one of the three splendid houses in the chestnut avenue, to elicit her help if a battle with Frank became unavoidable. It was the one thing, she told herself, snipping ferociously, for which she would fight. After all, Jeremy was her child – hers and John's – and she was determined to do the right thing by him.

A woman's voice broke upon her militant thoughts, and she turned to see her neighbour Winnie Bailey at the gate.

'And how is the doctor this morning?' enquired Phil, going towards her.

'Not too good today. He's up and down, as you know, and had a trying night. He's asleep now, and I thought I would slip down to Lulling for some meat while he's resting.'

'Shall I look in?'

'No, no, many thanks. Jenny's there till twelve, and I shan't be long. Anything I can fetch for you?'

'Nothing, thank you. Frank's at the office today and won't

be back until tomorrow. He's dining with an American editor and hoping to do a deal.'

'Good luck to him! So I suppose you and Jeremy are having boiled eggs?'

'Absolutely right! I'll start cooking again tomorrow.'

'Well, I must be off,' said Winnie, casting an anxious look at the doctor's bedroom window. 'He likes me to be there when he first wakes.'

She hurried away, and for the first time Phil thought how old and frail she looked. What a burden of anxiety she carried constantly! It put her own trivial worries into perspective, she thought.

And what a daily battle was being fought by the gallant doctor next door! It was a long and valiant campaign waged against the grimmest of all adversaries.

Sadly, as Phil and all Thrush Green knew, victory would have to be conceded to the enemy before long.

Playtime was over, and in the infants' room at the village school little Miss Fogerty sat at her desk with a small group of children gathered about her.

The rest of the class was engaged in various activities. Some of the children were copying sentences from the blackboard, others were reading at their tables, and the usual hard core of juvenile delinquents was making itself objectionable to the more law-abiding of its neighbours.

The group clustered by Miss Fogerty consisted of those who found reading difficult. In her young days, they would have been known as 'backward'. Halfway through her career, the term was changed to 'less able'. Now that she was nearing retirement, she believed such a group was called 'remedial'. The name might change, thought Miss Fogerty – the children did not. They provided her with the hardest session of her teaching day.

By dint of using every reading method known, she battled on day after day. Some, she knew, would never read, and would rely on television, radio, and the age-old practical methods of personal demonstration to acquire knowledge.

Others would gain enough mechanical skill to make out the headlines or to puzzle out where to sign a form. A very few would catch up with the rest of the class, and on these Miss Fogerty relied for any encouragement.

Grubby forefingers were descending the long cards made by Miss Fogerty years before.

'Per – in' they chanted, gazing at the picture beside the first word.

'Ter – in' they went on.

'Fer – in.' Really, thought Miss Fogerty, with pride, that fish was very well executed!

'Grer – in.' And that smile too! The cards had worn extremely well.

She stood up suddenly, and looked over the heads of her pupils to the back row of the classroom.

'Any more of that pinching, Johnny Dodd, and you will stay in after school.'

She sat down abruptly. The drone continued without interruption.

'Cher – in.'

She allowed her thoughts to wander. Miss Fogerty disliked change. She and Miss Watson, her headmistress, had held sway at Thrush Green School for many years, and were firm friends. But now, after all this time, a third teacher had been appointed, and although the term was yet young, Miss Fogerty could see signs that disturbed her.

For one thing, the girl was only just in her twenties, and though Miss Fogerty was fair-minded enough to see that this could not be helped – after all, the time of one's birth was beyond one's control – she realized that Miss Potter's view of teaching was quite different from her own and Miss Watson's.

And then she dressed in such a peculiar way, pondered Miss Fogerty, automatically replacing a wavering forefinger upon the reading card. If she were headmistress she would never allow a teacher in her school to wear a trouser suit. Most unbecoming. Most unladylike.

'But very practical, dear,' Miss Watson had said, in answer to Miss Fogerty's expressed doubts. 'And will keep the girl warm in that rather draughty new building.'

The new building, called colloquially 'the terrapin' was a purely functional classroom which had been erected at the farther end of the playground to house the young juniors. It was termed a temporary building, but Miss Fogerty and Miss Watson, with years of experience behind them, faced the fact that the terrapin would still be there long after they had retired.

The new housing estate, built along the road to Nod and Nidden, supplied most of the extra pupils at Thrush Green School. For generations the village school had accommodated about fifty or sixty children in its two rooms, but now that the number on roll had risen to over eighty, the third classroom had been deemed a positive necessity.

Miss Fogerty would dearly have loved to have the terrapin as her classroom. As soon as the building began, she put forward excellent reasons why the room should be put at the infants' disposal.

'You know how much noise they make,' she pointed out to Miss Watson. 'We shouldn't disturb anyone over there. And the cloakrooms and lavatories are all built in – so convenient for small children. You know how they bang the lobby door every time they need to go across the yard.'

'The room is far more suited to the needs of the juniors,' said her headmistress firmly.

'And then it's so sunny,' pleaded Miss Fogerty, 'and will bring on the mustard and cress and bean seeds and bulbs so beautifully. As well as being healthier for the babies.'

'All that applies to the junior class too,' pointed out Miss Watson obdurately. She used her trump card.

'Besides, Agnes,' she said, more gently, 'I should miss you. I like to think of you at my right hand.'

There was no answer to this, and Miss Fogerty gave way with her usual docility.

But the decision rankled. She would have liked a change. Hadn't she spent the best years of her life in the infants' room which faced north east and was decidedly shabby and dark? The fact that its main window overlooked Thrush Green, and thus afforded an interesting view of the comings and goings of its inhabitants, was a point in the classroom's favour, but even that could pall. It would have been lovely to have a new view looking across the little valley to Lulling Woods, and to have the sun streaming through that beautiful low window, so infinitely preferable to the high Gothic one which the Victorian architect had considered right and proper for the original building.

And although it was uncommonly nice of dear Miss Watson to say that she would miss her, pondered Miss Fogerty, would it not have been even nicer if she had taken her old friend's wishes into consideration? After all, she had loyally served Miss Watson and Thrush Green School through thick and thin, and had rarely asked for a favour. It would have been gratifying to think that those long years had been recognized and rewarded with a willingness to meet her request.

It would be easier to bear, Miss Fogerty considered, if Miss Potter had appreciated the new classroom, but there had been a great many grumbles from the newcomer about draughts, and glaring sunlight, and doors which stuck, and even about noisy lavatory cisterns, which Miss Fogerty thought privately it was indelicate to mention.

No, Miss Potter was not an asset to the staff, that was plain. Certainly, it was early days to judge, and maybe she would improve on acquaintance, and mellow a little in the company of two older and wiser women.

Nevertheless, that old tag about two being company and three none, had some horse sense. Things could never be quite the same between dear Miss Watson and herself with a third member of staff to consider.

A thought struck her. Of course if Miss Potter continued to be disgruntled about the terrapin, then she might prefer to take over her own room. And if that didn't suit, then the girl might apply for a post elsewhere. Heaven alone knew, a good teacher would be snapped up anywhere.

Miss Fogerty's spirits rose at the thought. She smiled upon her labouring readers.

'Very good,' she told them warmly. 'You've all tried hard this morning. Rose, collect the cards, and then take round the sweet tin. I am very pleased with you.'

3. Dotty Harmer's Legacy

True to his word, the Reverend Charles Henstock made a point of examining the churchyard of St Andrew's, with particular care, within the week.

He was not a man who responded to his surroundings with any great degree of sensitivity. On the whole, he was unobservant, and perhaps this was a blessing when one surveyed the gloomy setting of the rectory, and the cold and undistinguished interior of his church. Someone, a century earlier, had removed, with a heavy Victorian hand, any little prettinesses which St Andrew's once enjoyed, and put in a truly appalling reredos at much the same time as the iron railings had been erected upon the low Cotswold stone wall which Thrush Green had once thought adequate as a boundary.

There was no doubt about it, thought the rector, pacing the uneven paths between tilting tombstones, the place *was* neglected. He looked over the railings across the green, noticing for once how spruce it looked, how fine was the chestnut avenue in the morning sunlight, as the leaves began to turn from green to gold. The hedges and gardens were tidy. The hanging baskets, outside 'The Two Pheasants', were still ablaze with geraniums and lobelia plants. Only here, in this corner of Thrush Green, was there something shabby. The most hallowed spot of all, thought the rector, turning to survey it again, was the most shameful. Something would have to be done.

But what? He was debating the advisability of calling at Albert Piggott's cottage, when the sexton emerged from the vestry door. No doubt he had been checking the boiler fuel. Very soon it would be needed, and what an expense! Charles Henstock sighed as he approached Albert.

'Another lovely day, Albert.'

'Need some rain.'

'Surely not.'

'Runner beans is drying out.'

Albert passed on the information with morose relish. Albert hated optimists.

'I've been thinking about this churchyard, Albert. Do you happen to have heard of anyone to give you a hand?'

'Not a living soul. What about that bit you put in the paper? Any takers?'

'I fear not. It seems that no one wants this sort of work.'

'Can't blame 'em,' said Albert laconically. 'They gets more standing by some bit of machinery doin' dam' all.'

The rector decided to let the oath pass.

'Well, we must do something ourselves, I suppose. Mr Shoosmith suggested a working party to help you.'

Albert flushed an ugly red. If there was anything he hated more than optimists, it was newcomers putting their oar in where they wasn't needed. Cheek, coming into his church-yard!

'And what does this 'ere *working party* intend to do, may I ask?' he enquired, with heavy sarcasm.

The rector, who was no coward, spoke out.

'To cut the grass, straighten some of these tombstones, and get rid of that dreadful mess of weeds which has been an eyesore for months. That would be a start, anyway.'

Albert's anger now became tinged with self-pity. There was a decided whine in his tone when he replied.

'Well, that's all very fine and large, but a bit of tem'pry help don't go far. Since my operation I'm a sick man, as well you knows. It ain't that I'm not willing, but the flesh is weak, hacked about as I was by that ol' butcher Pedder-Bennett down the hospital.'

'You were extremely lucky,' said the rector severely, 'to have such a distinguished surgeon to operate on you. You might not have been here at all, if the Lulling Hospital staff had not worked so swiftly and so well.'

Albert did not reply, but turned to spit neatly behind the angel erected in pious memory of one Hepzibah Armstrong by her sorrowing husband. The rector, with Christian fortitude, restrained his temper.

'But that is exactly the point, Piggott,' he continued. 'We must rely on volunteer help. What else is there to do?'

'They used to have a few sheep in here in my Dad's time, to crop the grass. Be less bother than a lot of amachoors stamping about breaking things when I wasn't looking.'

The rector sighed.

'Well, we must think of every possible method, but the aim is plain and clear. We simply cannot have God's acre neglected like this. It is a disgrace to Thrush Green and an affront to all decent men, dead and alive. In the meantime, you must do the best you can, Piggott, and accept any help that we can muster.'

He strode to the gate, leaving Albert to digest this un-palatable morsel of news.

Working parties! Interfering old busybodies! Best cut across to 'The Two Pheasants' for half a pint, he decided, setting off in the direction of that hostelry with more energy than he had shown that morning.

The rector had just reached his front door, when a high-pitched hallooing caused him to turn.

There, at the gate, was Dotty Harmer, Thrush Green's most famous eccentric. She was scrabbling helplessly at the latch of the gate, pulling it, as always, when it needed to be pushed, and becoming more and more breathless with her exertions.

'Let me, Dotty,' called the rector, hurrying to her aid. Two magazines slipped from her grasp to the ground, and as she bent to retrieve them her hat fell off. To the rector's surprise, he saw that it had a piece of elastic attached to it, but he could not recall Dotty ever having such a thing under her chin, as his sisters used to have as children. A less polite man might have tried to satisfy his curiosity with a blunt question, but Charles refrained.

'Thank you, thank you, Charles dear,' babbled Dotty, preceding her host up the path. As usual, Dotty's stockings were in concertinas round her skinny legs. Although Charles was a married man, he was hazy about the mechanics of keeping stockings at the correct tension. Dimity, he believed, had some sort of thing called a suspender belt, but surely these days ladies wore thin pantaloons – 'tights' did they call them? – which must be much simpler than tethering one's leg coverings. Perhaps Dimity could have a word with Dotty about these delicate matters? It really must be most uncomfortable for Dotty to go about like this.

By now they had entered the hall, but almost immediately Dotty turned, voicing protests, and practically capsizing the rector.

'No, I didn't mean to come in! I won't come in!'

'But you *are* in,' pointed out Charles patiently. 'Come through to see Dimity.'

'Well, I mustn't stay,' said Dotty, turning round again, and resuming her progress with much agitation. 'I've so much to do before I go away.'

'Go away?' echoed Dimity, appearing at the kitchen door. 'What's all this about?'

'Oh, I'm not going for a day or two. As soon as it suits Connie, I shall be off.'

'I don't think I know Connie,' began Dimity.

'Connie? My Connie? You *must* know her! That niece of

mine with the red hair. Used to lisp as a child, but grew out of it, I'm thankful to say.'

'And you are going to stay with her?' enquired the rector. 'Do sit down, Dotty.'

Dotty's agitation doubled.

'No, no! I really must go,' she said, remaining rooted to the spot.

'But I should very much like to sit down,' replied Charles patiently, 'but I can't if you won't.'

'I don't see why not,' said Dotty, hitching up one of the cascading stockings. 'Your joints are all in order, I take it?'

'I was brought up to stand whilst ladies were standing,' smiled Charles, 'and somehow I still do so. So please sit down.'

Dotty thumped down into a kitchen chair, and the rector and his wife followed suit.

'Satisfied?' said Dotty.

'Thank you, yes,' said Charles, sighing with relief. 'I've been talking to Piggott, and I must say it is an exhausting activity.'

'That churchyard's a disgrace,' pronounced Dotty.

'I know. That's what I was discussing with Piggott. He tells me that a few sheep used to graze there years ago.'

Dimity looked alarmed.

'I shouldn't think the relatives of the dead there would care to have sheep roaming about.'

'Why on earth not?' demanded Dotty. 'Very sensible arrangement, I should say. But why sheep? Why not let my two goats have the run of the graveyard? They'd keep it down beautifully.'

It was now the rector's turn to look alarmed. Dotty in pursuit of an aim was a force to be reckoned with. As the daughter of a long-dead local schoolmaster, whose discipline was still spoken of with shuddering, Dotty's spirit was militant and tenacious.

'I could take them up each morning,' continued Dotty, waxing enthusiastic, 'and bring them back for afternoon milking time. Or even milk them there, of course. Ella could slip across for her daily pint much more conveniently.'

'But Dotty –' began Charles.

He was swept aside. Dotty in full spate had the same over-whelming force as the River Niger in that condition.

'Mind you, you'd have to remove those round metal grid things with everlasting flowers stuck in them. The dear girls would be bound to try and eat them, and even goats would find those indigestible. Marble chippings couldn't do much harm, I imagine. Simply provide roughage. But we'd better take away the plastic vases.'

'*I could not countenance goats in the churchyard,*' trumpeted Charles fortissimo.

Dotty looked flabbergasted.

'Then why countenance sheep?'

'I have not said that I would countenance *sheep*,' replied Charles, in his usual dulcet tones. 'All I said was that *once* – many years ago – sheep, so Piggott assured me, and he may well be wrong, knowing Piggott, were allowed to crop the grass.'

'It's nothing short of racial discrimination!' exclaimed Dotty. Her face was becoming very flushed.

Dimity hastily changed the subject.

'Tell me about Connie, dear. I think I remember her now.'

Dotty allowed herself to be side-tracked, but Charles had the uncomfortable feeling that she would return to the attack shortly.

'My brother's child. David, you remember? Died last spring?'

'Indeed I do.'

'Well, at last the lawyers have sorted things out – though why they take so long remains a mystery. David left a perfectly straightforward will. One or two small bequests to relatives and friends and the rest to Connie. A child of seven could have settled it during an afternoon, but here we are – months later – only just about to take possession. I'm going down to fetch my car.'

'Your car?'

'Yes, yes,' Dotty said testily.

She rose from the chair, dropping the magazines which she had been clutching the while.

'Thought I'd hand these in before I forgot them. Such a lot to do before setting off.'

'But can you drive?' asked Charles.

'Of course I can drive! I had a licence on my seventeenth birthday and I've always kept it up. Luckily, I shan't need to take a test.'

'But, Dotty dear,' said Dimity, 'I've never seen you driving, and I've known you for quite twenty years.'

'Maybe, but it's all in order, and the car is taxed and insured. I quite look forward to the drive back.'

Charles and Dimity exchanged looks of horror behind their departing guest's back.

Charles spoke with some authority.

'Dotty, do I understand that you propose to make the return journey alone?'

'Naturally. Go down by coach, back in the car. Simplicity itself.'

'Can't you get a garage to deliver it for you? Or Connie? You see, things have altered since your driving days. The traffic, for one thing. And then, cars are quite different now. You might not be able to control it.'

Dotty's face became quite puce with indignation.

'Not able to control it?' she echoed. 'If I could manage

Father's Studebaker and my dear little bull-nosed Morris, which tended to be temperamental, I don't mind admitting, then I can certainly drive David's car. Don't forget, I often sat in it when I was staying there. It was very easy to drive. David always said so.'

'Nevertheless,' said Charles, 'I think you should have someone with you. If need be, I will accompany you myself.'

'Rubbish! Stuff and nonsense!' exclaimed Dotty, making for the door. 'I never heard such a lot of fuss about nothing. I wish I hadn't told you about my little legacy.'

She began to storm along the corridor to the front door, Dimity following her.

'Don't be upset, Dotty dear, and do think over Charles's offer. And, by the way, what is Connie's address, just in case we want to get in touch while you're away?'

'The Limes, Friarscombe, will find me,' said Dotty, struggling with the front door.

'And perhaps we'd better have the telephone number,' continued Dimity, opening the door. 'Just in case the goats come to any harm, you know.'

Dotty, for a brief moment, remained motionless, as the full horror of this possibility burst upon her.

'Sensible, Dimity. Friarscombe Two One Three. I'll see you about, probably, before I go.'

She set off down the path without so much as one backward look. Her stockings, Charles noticed, were in a highly dangerous state of decline.

Dimity returned to the kitchen, looking determined.

'Charles, we must get in touch with Connie and see that Dotty is kept from driving that car alone.'

'I quite agree. She really wouldn't be safe.'

'And nor would anyone in her path,' added Dimity.

*

'Heard about Miss Harmer's car?' enquired Betty Bell of her employer the next morning.

'No,' said Harold, removing a glass ash tray, in the nick of time, from the path of Betty's onslaught with a duster.

'She told me yesterday while I was giving her kitchen a going over. And did it need it? She's got a great cardboard box standing on that dresser of hers – why, it's been there ever since I started doing for her, and that's how long?'

She stood transfixed, frowning with concentration. Harold took advantage of the lull to rescue *The Times* hoping to find a more peaceful spot in which to peruse it.

'Must be all of eight years,' announced Betty, coming to life again and attacking the mantelpiece.

'And this box is absolutely chocker with bits she's cut out of newspapers. One of 'em was over twenty years old! Think of that! I'm telling you!'

'I know you are,' said Harold patiently.

'Well, at last I got her to let me sort it out, only we didn't get far. Know why?'

'No.'

'There was a mouse's nest down the bottom.'

'Good heavens!' exclaimed Harold.

'Not a *modern* one,' said Betty comfortingly. 'A proper broken down old thing it was – no babies or that! But still, a nest, and all made of chewed up paper. Quite pretty really. Miss Harmer was all for taking it into the village school for the children to see but I said not. I could just see Miss Watson's face if Miss Harmer took that thing out and sprinkled mouse confetti all over the floor. Besides, it's me that has to clear it up.'

'What's this got to do with the car?'

'Only that she told me while we made a bonfire of all the kitchen muck. Her brother's left her his car and she's going to get it on Friday.'

'I didn't know she drove.'

'She don't. At least, she hasn't for donkey's years. We all used to rush up into the hedge when we was kids if old Dot – I mean Miss Harmer – was coming.'

'I expect someone will drive her back,' said Harold, anxious to get to grips with *The Times* crossword. A swift glance had shown him that 'dairy cats' could easily be turned into 'caryatids' at 6 across.

'Rather them than me!' replied his help. 'Not that there'll be any need. She's driving it herself.'

'Good Lord!' exclaimed Harold, suitably shaken, and made his escape.

By the time night fell upon Thrush Green, Dotty's news was common knowledge, and consternation was rife.

Doctor Lovell, Doctor Bailey's young assistant, told his wife Ruth about the projected trip by one of his more difficult patients.

'But she's a perfect menace!' cried Ruth. 'She once took Joan and me to a fête, and I wonder we ever got back alive. How father and mother ever came to give her permission, I can't think. We were about ten and eight, I suppose. I had nightmares for weeks afterwards.'

'She certainly hasn't driven since I came here,' said her husband. 'Do you think you could offer to drive the car back?'

'With Dotty in it? Panting to get her hands on the wheel? You don't know what you're asking,' cried Ruth with spirit. 'And the answer is a resounding "No!"'

Doctor Bailey shook his tired old head when Winnie told him about Dotty's car.

'The same angel that guards drunkards will guard Dotty,' he told her, smiling.

'It's other people I'm thinking of,' retorted Winnie.

At the rectory, Charles had telephoned to Connie at Friarscombe and put forward the fears of all at Thrush Green. The reply was not very satisfactory.

'I'll do my best,' said the distant voice, 'but you know Aunt Dot.'

Sadly, the rector agreed that he did indeed.

He put down the telephone and turned to his wife.

'One last hope – Ella,' he said. 'She drives, and she can sometimes persuade Dotty to do things when other people have failed.'

'I'll go over tomorrow morning,' promised Dimity.

She found her old friend in the garden. Ella was picking runner beans, and successfully trampling upon a row of carrots next in line.

'They'll survive,' was her answer to Dimity's protests. 'Want some beans? Enough here to feed an army. All or nothing with runners, isn't it?'

'I'd love some. I'll pick them.'

'No, you won't. There's ample in the basket.'

She led the way back to the path, stepping from carrot fronds to shallots and then on to the onion row. Dimity, wincing, picked her way after her.

Ella sat down heavily on the wooden seat by the back door, and began to remove her muddy shoes. Dimity sat beside her. The sun was already warm and she thought, yet again, what a wonderfully pleasant place the old cottage garden was. There was no such sheltered spot across at the rectory. She chided herself for disloyalty, and turned to Ella.

Her friend had produced the battered tobacco tin so familiar from times past. Ella began to roll one of her disreputable cigarettes.

'Well, what brings you over?' she asked, licking the edge of the paper.

'Dotty,' said Dimity. 'She's been left a car –'

'I know,' replied Ella, fumbling for matches.

'And she really can't drive, you know, and we're all so worried. Charles and I wondered if you could have a word with her, and persuade her to let you go with her –'

A cloud of pungent smoke polluted the morning air before Ella replied.

'You're too late, Dim my girl,' she said, slapping Dimity's thin thigh painfully. 'I saw her going down to catch the nine-thirty coach, case in hand.'

'But she said Friday!' cried Dimity, appalled. 'And to-day's Thursday!'

'I expect she got wind of all the fuss,' said Ella, 'and decided to get away while the going was good.'

She struggled to her feet and retrieved the basket.

'Can't say I blame her,' she puffed, her grizzled head now wreathed in blue smoke. 'Dotty knows her way around for all her scatter-brained ways.'

She began to lead the way to the kitchen.

'You mark my words,' said Ella, 'she'll arrive back at Thrush Green safe and sound. They say the devil looks after his own, don't they?'

Later, beans in hand, and Ella's dire words ringing in her head, Dimity returned to the rectory to break the news to Charles.

She refrained from quoting Ella exactly. At times, she felt, her old friend expressed herself rather too forcefully. The rector's comment was typical.

'We can only hope that Connie will be given strength to prevail. It will need great courage to oppose Dotty.'

'It will need more to drive with her!' retorted his wife with spirit.

4. Driving Trouble

The matter of St Andrew's churchyard continued to perplex the rector and the parochial church council.

At an emergency meeting it was decided to put up one or two notices in public spots asking for volunteers to help to tidy the graveyard. The rector also drafted a paragraph for inclusion in the parish magazine.

Reaction was varied, and mainly negative.

'What's old Piggott get paid for then?' queried one belligerently.

'He's past it,' said another, more kindly disposed.

'Then he should pack it in, and let someone else get the money,' retorted the first speaker.

'I reckons the council ought to keep it tidy. What do we pay rates for?' demanded another, reading the notice which Harold Shoosmith had pinned up in the bar of 'The Two Pheasants'.

'Don't talk daft!' begged a stout-drinker. 'It's got nothing to do with the council!'

'Well, I've been a Wesleyan all my life. I don't see why I should clean up for the C. of Es.'

'You'll be put in there, won't you?' demanded another. 'Whatever you be, you'll end up there. Why your old ma and pa are up agin the wall already! Don't matter what church or chapel we goes to, that's the common burial ground. I reckons we all ought to lend a hand.'

But not many agreed with the last speaker, and as he was a shepherd, bent and weatherbeaten, and now in his eighty-fifth year, he was not in a position to engage personally in the project.

The rector, experienced in the ways of men, was not surprised at the lack of response, although he was disappointed.

'It seems sad,' he said to Harold Shoosmith, 'that none of the younger men has offered. In fact, the only people willing to do anything are you, and Percy Hodge, the farmer, and myself.'

'I really thought we might get some volunteers from the new housing estate at Nod,' replied Harold. 'Plenty of able-bodied chaps up there.'

'They have their new gardens to see to,' said Charles charitably. 'And most of them do over-time, you know, to make ends meet. They are rather hard-pressed. It's quite understandable.'

'You're a good deal more forgiving than I am,' said Harold. 'Young Doctor Lovell told me he could offer an evening a week, and if he can, then why can't others?'

'Better one willing fighter than ten men press-ganged into the battle,' replied the rector philosophically.

'I suppose you're right. We muster at the church gate next Wednesday then?'

'At six, my dear fellow. What a blessing the evenings are still light! Piggott will be there to help.'

And to make sure we know our place, thought Harold, watching his friend's receding figure.

'Coffee up!' shouted Betty Bell, as he re-entered his house. 'Want it here or on your own?' Sometimes, when Betty gave him just such a comradely salute, he found himself thinking of the obsequious native boys who had waited upon him for so many years, with deference and respect. Or had they perhaps, simply acted a part? In any case, it was no good harking back. Times had changed.

'I'll have it with you,' said Harold, entering the kitchen. Two cups steamed on a tray, and a plate held some dark sticky gingerbread.

'Have a bit,' said Betty, pushing the plate towards him. 'It's a present for you.'

'Very kind,' said Harold, looking at it doubtfully.

Betty broke into a peal of laughter.

'You're thinking Miss Harmer sent it! Well, she didn't. I made it myself.'

'Then I should love a piece, Betty,' said Harold, smiling.

'You don't think I'd let you eat anything *she'd* made, do you? No disrespect, mark you – Miss Harmer's a real lady, I always say – but that kitchen of hers is a right old muddle, and you'd as likely get bird seed or Karswood powder in your cake as not.'

'It's delicious,' nodded Harold.

'Seen her car yet?'

'No. She drove it back herself, after all, I suppose?'

'Between you and me, that's what she wants Thrush Green to think, but actually that niece of hers drove most of the way. They came back that night, and her Connie got Reg Bull's taxi from Lulling to take her back, as soon as she'd had a bite.'

'But why the secrecy? And why didn't the young lady stay the night?'

'Miss Harmer's proud, see. Didn't like to let on that she'd never driven herself home, after all she'd said. And that Connie's like her auntie. She's got all manner of animals to look after, so she had to get back.'

'I see.'

'Besides,' went on Betty, beginning to stack the china swiftly, 'would you want to stay the night with Miss Harmer?'

Harold assumed that this was a rhetorical question, and forbore to answer.

'You'd never know what was in your bed,' said Betty. 'I've known the time the cat had kittens there, under the eiderdown, and Miss Harmer wouldn't hear of them being moved for days. Some people don't like that sort of thing, you know. We haven't all got Miss Harmer's funny ways.'

Harold nodded agreement.

'But what about the car? No one has seen her in it yet.'

'She's been out in it all right. Got some petrol from Reg Bull's, 'cos my nephew served her, but she's only took it round the lanes, testing it a bit, I reckon.'

'It sounds as though she is being very sensible,' said Harold, rising. 'She's bound to feel that she needs a little practice after such a long time without a car.'

'It isn't *practice* she wants,' said Betty downrightly. 'It's a chauffeur.'

She deposited the china in the washing-up bowl, and Harold escaped.

It so happened that Harold was vouchsafed the vision of Dotty Harmer at the wheel, the very next afternoon. He was standing outside his front gate, contemplating some dwarf marigolds. Should he pull them up in readiness for planting the wallflowers, or should he enjoy their colour for another week or two?

Since his return to England, some few years earlier, he found that such problems occurred regularly. Was it his imagination, or did the Spring in his boyhood start earlier, and finish, in a tidy fashion, in good time to put in the summer bedding plants? Now, it seemed, it remained cold in June, and everything was proportionately later. These dwarf marigolds, for instance, had only come into flower a few weeks ago, he told himself, and yet, if he wanted to get the beds dug over and the wallflowers established, then they really should be removed now.

He had just decided to grant them a reprieve for a week or two, facing the fact that by that time continuous rain, no doubt, would frustrate any gardening whatsoever, when he became conscious of a cacophony of horn-blowing coming from the steep hill which led from Thrush Green to Lulling.

Harold strode over to the green, and stood by the statue of his hero, Nathaniel Patten, the better to see the cause of the fuss. The main road, leading northward to the midlands, appeared to be free from traffic. Whatever the obstruction was, which was causing such irritation to so many drivers, was out of sight.

Harold continued to wait. The children from the village school, just let out to play, crowded against the railings behind him like so many inquisitive monkeys.

Albert Piggott appeared on his doorstep. Joan Young, girt in her gardening apron, came across the chestnut avenue, trowel in hand, to join Harold, and at least a dozen twitching curtains told of more sightseers.

'Do you think there's been an accident?' asked Joan. 'Perhaps we should run over.'

Even as she spoke, a small car, jerking spasmodically, came into view. It was impossible to see, at that distance, who held the wheel, but Harold guessed, correctly, who it might be.

'Dotty!' cried Harold and Joan in unison, setting off across the grass at a brisk pace.

The car had come to another stop, by the time they arrived, just outside Ella Bembridge's house. Behind it stretched a long queue, the end of it out of sight in the main street of Lulling. Immediately behind Dotty's small vehicle was a Land-Rover towing a horse-box.

'Get the bloody thing off the road!' shouted the driver. His face was scarlet with wrath, as he leant out of the side window. 'Dam' women drivers! No business to have a licence!'

Further protestations came from those behind, and the

additional music of car horns rent the air.

Dotty, peering agitatedly at the car pedals, was pink herself, and very cross indeed.

'Here,' said Harold, wrenching open the door, 'hop out, Miss Harmer, and I'll park her in the side road.'

'Why should I get out?' demanded Dotty. 'And what right have you to order me out of my own carriage, may I ask?'

'Pull the old besom out,' begged the Land-Rover driver. He began to open his door, and Harold feared that battle would be joined.

'*Please*,' he pleaded. 'You see, there is such a long queue, and this road is far too narrow here to overtake safely. I'm afraid that the police will be along to see what's happening.'

'*You* may be afraid of the police,' said Dotty sharply, 'but I am *not*. Now kindly take your hand from the door.'

'But – ' began Harold, but could not continue, as, by some miracle of combustion the engine had started again into spasmodic life and Dotty moved slowly, in a succession of convulsive jerks, into the side road leading to the church. There was a mild explosion, a puff of smoke, the car stopped, and Dotty put forth her deplorably-stockinged legs and got out.

'Stick to your bike, lady!' shouted the Land-Rover man rudely, as he quickened his pace along the main road. A few imprecations, some shaken fists and vulgar gestures were directed towards Dotty as other cars passed, but most of the drivers contented themselves with resigned glances as they glimpsed the scarecrow figure of the one who was responsible for their delay.

The three waited until the last of the queue vanished northwards, before speaking.

'Would you allow me to have a look at the car?' asked Harold.

'Of course, of course,' said Dotty airily, as if washing her hands of the whole affair.

At this moment, Ella appeared and crossed the road.

'What on earth have you been up to, Dotty? Never heard such a racket since just before D-day when we had all those tanks rumbling through.'

'I simply drove quietly from West Street up the hill here. Just because I do not care to *scorch* along, this queue formed behind me. I had some difficulty in changing gear at the bottom, I must admit, but there was no need for the vulgar demonstration of impatience which you have just witnessed. No manners anywhere these days! A pity some of these men weren't taught by my father. He wouldn't have spared the strap, I can tell you!'

Harold climbed out of the car and came towards them.

'It's quite a simple problem,' he said. 'The petrol's run out.'

'The *petrol?*' echoed Dotty. 'But we only filled it when we brought the car from Connie's, not ten days ago!'

'Nevertheless, it's empty now.'

'But how can you tell?' demanded Dotty. 'You didn't put in your dip stick.'

'There's a little gauge on the dashboard,' explained Harold patiently. 'Perhaps you would allow me to show you?'

'Don't trouble,' said Dotty, setting off towards the car. 'I'll just push her round, if you'll give me a hand, and coast down the hill to Reg Bull's for some fuel.'

'But it's not allowed!' cried Joan.

'You'll stop half way along the High Street, Dot.'

Dotty looked coldly at her old friend.

'I suppose there are still plenty of people capable of *pushing* me along to Reg Bull's,' she said witheringly. 'It's little enough to ask.'

Harold took command. Years of administration in far-flung corners of the world stood him in good stead.

'I have a spare gallon of petrol in my garage, and I shall put it into your tank, Miss Harmer. That should get you home safely, and then you can fill up next time you are out.'

'And while Harold's doing that,' said Ella, 'you can come and see my parsley. You know you said you wanted a root to take you through the winter.'

'Very well, very well,' muttered Dotty, allowing herself to be led away.

Joan Young accompanied Harold back across the green. Her expression was troubled.

'You know, she really shouldn't be allowed to drive that car.'

'I absolutely agree,' said Harold, 'but what's to be done?'

'I don't know, but I feel sure there's going to be some awful accident if Dotty is going to drive around these parts.'

'That might be a blessing in disguise,' said Harold, opening his gate. 'If she had to go to court she might be taken off the road for a while.'

'Let's hope it doesn't come to that,' exclaimed Joan.

'There was a lot to be said,' remarked Harold reflectively, 'for a man with a red flag going ahead of a car in the early days of motoring.'

'Dotty could do with one,' laughed Joan, 'but I wouldn't volunteer for the job if I were you.'

'No fear!' said Harold, making for the garage.

5. Skirmishes at the Village School

The serenity of September gave way to a blustery October, and Thrush Green was spattered with dead leaves.

The chestnut avenue shed its massive leaves, brown and crisp as cornflakes, and the children of Thrush Green School spent every available minute scuffling about happily, looking for conkers brought down by the wind. It was as much as their life was worth to throw sticks up into the branches to bring down the coveted nuts, for Miss Watson and Miss Fogerty, not to mention the occupants of the three houses which faced the avenue, kept a sharp eye on offenders and delivered swift punishment. Legend had it that a long-dead gardener, by the name of Dobb, had once clouted a young malefactor caught in the act of stick-throwing, with such severity, that he had been taken to Lulling Hospital with mild concussion. In such a rough and ready way had the beauty of Thrush Green's avenue been maintained over the years by those who loved it.

One tempestuous morning, the three teachers of Thrush Green School were sipping their tea in the infants' room and watching the school at play in the windswept playground.

It was young Miss Potter's turn for playground duty, but she continued to stand in Miss Fogerty's room, out of the weather, and enjoy her tea in comparative peace.

Miss Fogerty found this irritating for two reasons. In the first place, the girl's duty was to patrol the playground, no matter how inclement the weather, and to keep an eye on her charges.

Secondly, this was one of the few occasions when she could have had Miss Watson's attention, without the unwelcome presence of this newcomer. There were one or two little matters, such as the disappearance of the emergency knickers from the lower shelf of the infants' cupboard, which she needed to discuss with her headmistress. Miss Fogerty did not care to embark on the subject of knickers – even infants' knickers – with Miss Potter present. There was a coarse streak in the girl, Miss Fogerty feared, which might lead to some ribaldry – a thing which Miss Fogerty detested.

'Could I have some more coloured tissue paper from the stock cupboard?' asked Miss Potter.

'Of course, my dear,' replied Miss Watson. 'If I give you the key, you can help yourself.'

Miss Fogerty drew in her breath sharply. To be given a free hand in that holy of holies was something which she herself had never been granted, and which she would certainly never have expected.

Miss Watson, rummaging in her large handbag, produced a bunch of keys, indicated one, and handed over the bunch.

'Thanks,' said Miss Potter perfunctorily. 'I'll bob along now, I think.'

At that moment a piercing wail from outside the window called attention to some infant misdemeanour.

Miss Watson looked hastily at the wall clock, and remembered her responsibilities.

'You should be in the playground,' she said. 'Get the paper afterwards.'

'OK,' said Miss Potter, moving languidly towards the door. Miss Fogerty felt her cheeks flushing with anger. OK indeed! And to her own headmistress!

'Really!' she exclaimed as Miss Potter vanished, 'I don't know what the world is coming to!'

Miss Watson smiled indulgently.

'Times change, Agnes dear, and you must remember that not all teachers had the advantage of your excellent upbringing.'

Miss Fogerty, who had been looking, for all the world, like a little ruffled sparrow, allowed her feathers to be smoothed.

Head teachers, if they are worth their salt, are past masters of such diplomacy.

The wailing, it transpired, came from young Jeremy Prior, the son of Phil Hurst by her first marriage.

Miss Potter led the child into the lobby, glad to be once again out of the bitter wind. Her charge, still weeping, bled profusely from his right knee, and studied two scratched palms through his tears.

'It will soon be better,' said Miss Potter. 'We'll just wash you clean.'

'I will do the washing,' said a stern voice.

Miss Fogerty had entered the lobby, and now advanced upon the pair.

'Your place,' she said firmly, 'is in the playground. I will look after Jeremy. After all, he is in my class. You'd better hurry outside again before there are any more accidents!'

Miss Potter tossed her unkempt head and sniffed contemptuously. Interfering old busybody! Always got her knife into me! Her gestures communicated her feelings as plainly as if she had spoken, but little Miss Fogerty remained unmoved.

She fetched the first-aid box, and sat down by the tearful boy on the shoe lockers. She had never seen Jeremy crying before. He was a tough, cheerful child, who got on well with his classmates.

'How did it happen?' she asked, dabbing gently at the grazed knee with wet cotton wool.

'Johnny Dodd tripped me up,' said Jeremy, trying not to wince.

'Then I shall have something to say to Johnny Dodd,' replied Miss Fogerty.

The dabbing continued. A weak solution of antiseptic liquid was applied, and finally Miss Fogerty began to cut lint and unroll bandages.

Jeremy, whose tears had now ceased, watched with some alarm.

'Will it stick?' he asked tremulously.

'Hardly at all,' said Miss Fogerty, combining comfort with honesty. She remembered, all too clearly, her own broken knees in childhood, and the horror of soaking off bandages made of old clean linen sheeting. She felt great sympathy for the little boy. He had endeared himself to her from the first, and she wondered now if it might not be a good thing to take him to his home across the green, for the rest of the morning.

Permission, of course, must be obtained from Miss Watson.

'Is mummy at home?' she enquired, rolling the bandage deftly round the quivering leg.

'Yes. She waved to me when I was playing just now.'

Miss Fogerty slit the end of the bandage and made a neat bow.

'Go into the classroom and keep warm. I'll be back in a minute.'

She found Miss Watson in her room, and told her what had occurred.

Miss Watson's face began to assume a stern expression. Miss Fogerty knew, from long experience, that her headmistress was in one of her 'What-will-the-office think?' moods.

She moved swiftly to the attack.

'I think it's one of those occasions when you can afford to be lenient,' said Miss Fogerty, with unwonted determination. 'After all, if you can stretch a point about fetching our own stock from the cupboard, I should think Jeremy could be sent home to get over the shock for a couple of hours. He will be back this afternoon, I have no doubt.'

Miss Watson gazed sharply at her assistant. Her glance took in the militant gleam in Miss Fogerty's normally mild eye.

She answered with due deference.

'As you think best, Agnes dear. You know I have every confidence in your judgement.'

She watched the little figure wheel about and march towards her own classroom.

Miss Watson sighed, and turned to face her reflection in the dusky glass of 'The Light of the World', behind her desk, which served as a somewhat unsatisfactory mirror.

She patted her hair into place in readiness for the return of her class.

'I must walk warily with dear Agnes,' she told herself. 'Even worms will turn!'

Mrs Hurst, thought Miss Fogerty, behaved perfectly when she presented her with her wounded son a few minutes later.

'Hello, then,' she said, in some surprise. 'You've been in the wars, I see.'

She bent to give him a swift kiss and led him and his teacher indoors out of the wind.

'How very kind of you to bring him,' she said to Miss Fogerty. 'Do sit down.'

'I really musn't stop,' said Miss Fogerty, glancing around her at the chintz covers, the table littered with papers and the typewriter open and in use. A log fire burnt in the grate, and a cat was stretched before it warming its stomach blissfully. How snug it all looked!

She explained about the accident and how it had seemed best to let Jeremy come home at once.

'He was very brave,' she said.

Jeremy's answering smile touched her heart.

'I cried a bit,' he told his mother.

'Hardly at all,' said Miss Fogerty stoutly. 'A very brave boy.'

She turned towards the door.

'And now I must hurry back. My class has some work to do, but I don't want Miss Watson to have to keep an eye on the children for too long. She has enough to do with her own class.'

Phil accompanied her to the door, repeating her thanks.

'He'll be quite fit to come this afternoon, I feel sure,' she said.

'I *must* go,' said Jeremy. 'It's my day to fill in the weather-chart.'

'Then that settles it,' agreed his mother, exchanging glances with his teacher.

'Then I'll see you at two o'clock,' said Miss Fogerty, as Phil opened the front door.

They both started back. For there, about to ring the bell, was Winifred Bailey, the doctor's wife from next door, and there were tears on her cheeks.

Miss Fogerty was the first to collect herself. She acknowledged the doctor's wife, made swift farewells and set off briskly across the green.

'Not Donald?' queried Phil.

'I'm afraid so, and my telephone's out of order. I must get young Lovell immediately. He's in a very poor way.'

'Shall I go into him while you ring?'

'No, no, my dear. Jenny's there, and I'll go straight back.'

Phil left her by the telephone, and took the child into the kitchen, so that Winifred might have a little privacy.

'What's the matter with the doctor?' asked Jeremy, in far too loud a voice for his mother's liking.

'We don't know. That's why Doctor Lovell's coming.'

'But if he's a doctor,' began Jeremy.

'Hush, hush, for pity's sake,' pleaded his mother. 'Come and change your shoes, and help me to make an omelette for lunch.'

She was beating eggs when Winifred came into the kitchen. The older woman looked less strained.

'Thank you, Phil. He's coming immediately. I'll let you know how he gets on.'

Phil followed her to the door.

'*Please*,' she begged, 'let me do anything to help. I could take a turn at watching him or –'

Winifred put her hand on the girl's arm.

'You would be the first person I should turn to,' she assured her, before hurrying down the path.

Little Miss Fogerty, returning briskly to her duties across the wet grass of Thrush Green, was both excited and saddened by the scene which she had just witnessed.

It is always exhilarating to be the first to know of something of note, particularly in a small community, and Miss Fogerty's quiet life held little excitement.

On the other hand her grief for Doctor Bailey's condition was overwhelming. He had attended her for many years, and she remembered, with gratitude, his concern for her annual bouts of laryngitis which were, fortunately, about the only troubles for which she had to consult him.

His most valuable quality, Miss Fogerty considered, was his way of making one feel that there was always plenty of time, and that he truly wished to hear about his patient's fears and perplexities. It was this quality, above all others, which had so endeared the good doctor to Thrush Green and its environs. He had always been prepared to give – of his time, of his knowledge, and of his humour. His reward had been outstanding loyalty and affection.

Miss Fogerty pushed open the school door to be confronted by Miss Potter. Her arms were full of sheets of tissue paper in various colours, and her expression was unbearably smug, to Miss Fogerty's eyes.

She held the door open for the girl to pass. Miss Potter, without a word of thanks, allowed the older woman to shut it behind her, and made her way across the playground to the terrapin.

Miss Fogerty seethed with a mixture of emotions, but remained outwardly calm as she returned to her classroom.

The children were virtuously quiet. The door between the two rooms was propped open with a waste paper basket, and Miss Fogerty put her head into the neighbouring room to express her thanks and to report back on duty.

Miss Watson gave her a friendly smile and said that the children had been no trouble at all.

Miss Fogerty, bursting with the news she had so recently acquired, would have liked to tell Miss Watson all. In the old days, there would have been no hesitation. Out it would have come with a rush, and Miss Watson would have nodded gravely, as became a headmistress, and advised secrecy until the tidings were confirmed elsewhere, and both ladies would have felt pleasantly important, and with a strong bond of self-imposed propriety uniting them.

But the memory of Miss Potter, laden with goodies from the stock cupboard, checked Miss Fogerty's natural loquacity. She did not feel inclined to share this delicious tit-bit with her headmistress. She still smarted from the favours shown to that detestable Miss Potter. Let Miss Watson find out for herself, and then, when she told her assistant the news, Miss Fogerty would have the exquisite pleasure of saying, in as off-hand a manner as she could produce, that she had known for some time.

She sat down at her own desk and surveyed the orderly rows of tables with unseeing eyes.

Her heart was troubled. How *could* she, Agnes Fogerty, respected teacher at Thrush Green School for over thirty years, behave in such a despicable way! What would dear Mr Henstock say if he could read her mind at the moment? And were her thoughts worthy of the high ideals which had always directed the conduct of poor Doctor Bailey, now so near his end?

It was a terrible thing to find that one could become so mean and so petty. And so unhappy too, thought poor Miss Fogerty.

But, unhappy as she was, and torn with remorse and self-disgust, she knew that it was impossible to feel for Miss Watson that warm respect and friendliness which had meant so much to her for so long.

If only Miss Potter had never come to Thrush Green! If only Miss Potter were not here! If only Miss Potter would go!

The clock hands stood at twelve o'clock. Sighing, little Miss Fogerty stood for grace, and thanked God for blessings received, with a heavy heart.

On the way into the lobby, Johnny Dodd, arch-male-factor of the infants' class, whispered to his neighbour:

'We was quiet all that time and she never give us so much as a pear drop out of the sweet-tin!'

Injustice rankles at any age.

6. Doctor Bailey's Last Battle

Before nightfall, the news that Doctor Bailey was sinking was common knowledge at Thrush Green.

There was general sadness. Even Albert Piggott had a good word to say for the dying man, as he drank his half-pint of bitter at 'The Two Pheasants'.

'Well, we shan't see his like again,' he commented morosely. 'He done us proud, the old gentleman. I s'pose now we has to put up with young Doctor Lovell dashing in and out again before you can tell him what ails you.'

'There's the new chap,' said the landlord. 'Seems a nice enough young fellow.'

'Him?' squeaked Albert. 'Nothing but a beardless boy! I wouldn't trust my peptic ulcer to him, that I wouldn't. No, I'll put me trust in strong peppermints while I can, and hope Doctor Lovell can spare a couple of minutes when I'm real hard-pressed. You mark my words, we're all going to miss the old doctor at Thrush Green.'

It was the older people who were the saddest. Doctor Bailey had brought their children into the world, and knew the family histories intimately. He had not been active in the partnership for some years now, so that the younger inhabitants were more familiar with Doctor Lovell, who had married a Thrush Green girl, and was accepted as a comparatively worthy successor to Doctor Bailey.

But it was the old friends and neighbours, the Youngs, the Henstocks, Ella Bembridge, Dotty Harmer, the Hursts next door and the comparative newcomer, Harold Shoosmith, who were going to miss Donald Bailey most keenly. Most of them had visited the invalid often, during the past few months, marvelling at his gallant spirit and his unfailing good temper.

Now, as the day waned, their thoughts turned to that quiet grey house across the green. The rector had called during the afternoon and found Winnie Bailey sitting by her husband's bedside.

He was asleep, his frail hands folded on the white sheet. A downstairs room, once his study, had been turned into a bedroom for the last few months, and his bed faced the french windows leading into the garden he loved so well. Propped up on his pillows, he had enjoyed a view of the flower beds and the comings and goings at the bird-table all through the summer.

His particular joy was the fine copper beech tree which dominated the scene. He had watched it in early May, as the tiny breaking leaves spread a pinkish haze over the magnificent skeleton. He had rejoiced in its glossy purplish mid-summer beauty which had sheltered the gentle ring-doves that cooed among its branches. And now, in these last few days, he had watched its golden leaves fluttering down to form a glowing carpet at its foot, as the autumn winds tossed the great boughs this way and that.

For once, the boisterous wind was lulled. Wisps of high grey cloud scarcely moved behind the copper beech. The garden was very still, the bird-table empty, the room where the dying man lay as quiet and tranquil as the grave to which so soon he would be departing.

Charles Henstock sat beside his old friend for a short time, his lips moving in prayer. After a little he rose, and Winnie went with him into the sitting-room. She was calm and dry-eyed, and Charles admired her control.

'He's very much in our thoughts and prayers, as you know,' said Charles. 'I know that Ella and Dimity – everyone in fact – will want to know how he is and would like to call, but they don't wish to intrude at a time like this. Shall I tell them the latest news? Or would you like one of us to sit with you?'

Winnie smiled.

'You tell them, please. Doctor Lovell says it is only a matter of hours now. I shall stay by him. He has a few lucid moments every now and again. Why, he's even doing the crossword, bit by bit, but I think visitors would tire him too much. I know that they will understand.'

Charles nodded.

'Jenny is with me,' continued Winnie. 'She insisted on staying today, and I'm grateful to have someone here to answer the door. I will keep in touch, Charles dear, and I'll tell Donald you called.'

The sun was setting as the rector set off homeward. Long shadows stretched across the grass from the chestnut avenue and the houses round the green. Above 'The Two Pheasants' a curl of blue smoke hung in the still air. The bar fire had been lit ready for the customers.

Willie Bond, the postman, was pushing his bicycle along the road to Nidden, at the end of his last delivery, and in the distance the rector could see Ella vanishing down the alley that led to Lulling Woods and Dotty Harmer's house. No doubt, she was off to collect her daily pint of goat's milk.

Sad though he felt, there was a touch of comfort in these manifestations of life going on as usual. Donald Bailey, he knew, would agree with him. He remembered his philosophy so clearly. We are born, we live out little lives, we die. Our lives are cut to the same pattern, touching here, overlapping there, and thus forming rich convolutions of colour and shape. But at the end, we are alone, and only in the lives and memories of our children, our friends and our work can we hope to be remembered.

Charles Henstock, whose belief in an after-life was

absolute, had never been able to persuade his old friend to share his convictions, and he had once told Donald, after an amicable exchange of views on the subject, that he considered the doctor to be the finest unbeliever he had been privileged to meet.

In some ways, thought the rector, observing the cock on St Andrew's spire gilded with the setting sun, one could have no better epitaph.

A few minutes later, Harold Shoosmith walked through the chestnut avenue to post his letters at the box on the corner.

At the same time, Frank Hurst's car came up the hill and turned into the drive of Tullivers, next door to Doctor Bailey's.

He got out of the car and hailed his old friend. Harold thrust his letters in the box, and turned to meet Frank who was hobbling towards him.

'Rheumatism, Frank?'

'No, just stiff with driving. The traffic gets worse. I've been over two hours getting home.'

'You want to retire.'

'I will as soon as I can. Come in and have a drink. Phil would love to see you.'

They walked up the path, Harold glancing at the next house, but there was no movement there, except for the thread of smoke which hung above the chimney.

'Phil!' called Frank. 'I've brought Harold in for a drink.'

His wife came hurrying from the kitchen. Harold thought that she looked prettier than ever, and envied Frank the welcoming kiss. Once, for a short time, he himself had wondered if he might ask Phil to marry him, but it had come to naught, and looking at their happiness now, he felt glad for them, and relieved for himself that he still had his bachelor independence.

'What news of the doctor?' asked Frank. 'Any improvement since yesterday?'

Phil told him of Winnie's visit.

'I'm afraid he's on his way out,' said Harold. 'Thrush Green won't be the same without him.'

'I only hope that Winnie decides to stay,' said Phil. 'She has a sister somewhere in Cornwall who wants her to join forces with her, I know. They get on quite well, but . . .'

Her voice trailed away.

'As you say,' agreed Harold, holding up his sherry to admire its glow in the dying rays of the sun. 'People will make decisions when they are still in a state of shock. Not that I think Winnie will do anything so foolish. She's the most level-headed female I've ever met.'

At this moment Jeremy entered bearing a saucer.

'Hello, young man. Are you bringing us nuts or crisps?' asked Frank.

'Can't find them, so I've brought you some of my jelly babies,' said Jeremy, offering them to Harold.

'That's extremely generous of you,' said Harold politely. 'May I have a red one?'

'Not for me, thanks,' said his stepfather hastily.

'Not even a head? I'll eat the rest.'

'Not just now, my boy.'

His eye fell upon the bandage round the child's knee.

'Hello, what's this? A hospital job?'

'I fell over in the playground,' explained Jeremy. He deemed it wiser not to mention the infidelity of Johnny Dodd. He had been ticked off once before for telling tales.

'And Miss Fogerty brought me home,' continued the child, 'and I missed the last lesson at school this morning.'

Frank gave a quick enquiring look at his wife, Harold observed.

'Oh, nothing serious – just a graze. I think Miss Fogerty was glad to have him looked after for that half-hour. It bled quite a bit, you know.'

'You're a lucky chap,' said Frank. 'You won't be spoiled like this when you go off to boarding school.'

'Well, we won't talk about that just now,' said Phil hastily, and Harold thought that she had become rather pink. This was obviously a sore point at the moment.

He drained his glass, and heaved himself out of the armchair.

'Well, I must be getting back. Many thanks for the restorative. By the way, Charles is going to let us know how things go next door, so he told me. Shall I ring you?'

'Please do,' said Phil. 'I think he left there a few minutes ago.'

Harold made his farewells, and returned across the darkening green.

'I wonder who will win that particular skirmish?' he thought, remembering the faces of Frank and his wife, whilst Jeremy looked from one to the other.

At the gate, he turned and looked once more at the Baileys' house. A soft light in the doctor's downstairs bedroom made a golden square in the dusky stone of the house.

There was, alas, no doubt who would win the battle there.

The same subject was the topic of conversation between Ella Bembridge and Dotty Harmer, in the latter's cluttered kitchen near Lulling Woods.

'Jolly sad,' boomed Ella, 'snuffing it like that. The end of everything, I suppose.'

Dotty, scrabbling for change in a jar which, long ago, had held Gentlemen's Relish, gave a snort.

'If you were a true Christian, Ella, you would look upon it as a new beginning.'

'But who's to know?' Ella's voice was almost a wail.

Dotty looked at her friend sharply.

'Well, I, for one, know! If my dear father believed in the hereafter, and all the good and intelligent clergymen we have met in our lives do so too, then I am *quite confident.*'

'But what do you think happens, Dotty?'

'We are simply translated,' said Dotty briskly. She looked at the coins in her hand.

'Are you giving me five pence or five Ps for the milk? I quite forget.'

'It started at sixpence, if you remember, but now things have got so out of hand I thought you ought to have five Ps.'

'But isn't that a shilling? That's far too much.'

'The milkman charges more than that for his homogenized muck, so take the bob, Dotty dear, and we'll all be content.'

'It's more than generous. And I shan't have to bother with change, shall I?'

'No. And now, how do you mean *translated*? Drift off into other new babies, d'you mean, or daffodils, or wireworms? Some other form of life, as it were?'

Dotty grew scarlet with impatience.

'Of course not. I've no time for all that wishy-washy muddled thinking! When you die you simply leave your worn-out body behind, and your spirit takes off. Don't you ever pay attention to the teachings of the Church?'

'But takes off to *where*, Dotty?'

'To heaven, of course,' said Dotty tartly, seizing an enormous wooden spoon and advancing upon an iron saucepan which had been rumbling and grumbling to itself throughout the conversation.

'And don't fuss any more about such things,' said Dotty. 'I really haven't time to explain it all when the chickens are waiting to be fed.'

'Quite,' agreed Ella, taking up the goat's milk. 'It makes me sad, though, to think that we shan't see Donald Bailey again.'

'Speak for yourself,' replied Dotty, stirring furiously. 'I have every expectation of seeing the dear man again, in a better world.'

'That must be a comfort,' rejoined Ella, as she shut the kitchen door behind her.

'But not for me,' she added sadly to herself, setting off homeward through the twilight.

Donald Bailey stirred, and opened his eyes.

'Hello, my dear,' he said to Winnie. 'What's the time?'

'Six o'clock.'

'Good heavens! I must have slept most of the afternoon.'

He began to struggle to sit up, and Winnie helped him into a more upright position against the pillows.

'I feel all the better for the doze,' he said. 'Let's have another look at the crossword. It's almost done.'

She put the paper on his knees, and the pen in his hand.

'Only my specs,' he said, smiling. 'I'm worse than a baby. Poor Winnie! What a lot of work I make for you!'

'Rubbish,' said his wife. 'Would you like a drink?'

'Nothing, thanks. But have you eaten?'

'I haven't felt hungry.'

'But you must, my dear. I prescribe a light repast for you immediately, and eaten here where I can watch you.'

Winnie laughed.

'Well, I might make some coffee. Will you be all right for a minute or two?'

'Of course,' said the doctor, with a contented sigh. 'Just look at the top of the beech tree! Absolutely on fire in the setting sun. What a perfect sight!'

She left him marvelling at it.

As she hurried to the kitchen, it was Jenny's welfare that was engaging her attention at the moment. Had she helped herself to food? She doubted it.

Jenny had worked for the Baileys for several years. She came two or three mornings a week, from the other end of Lulling, on a decrepit bicycle. Her home was in a maze of alleyways in one of the most ancient and dilapidated quarters of the town. She looked after her aged foster-parents, Becky and Bill Fuller, who had taken her in as a little girl of ten.

They had been strict, honest and hard-working. The child had been pitied by neighbours for having 'a lean time of it'. But Jenny never complained. She was grateful to the couple for a home, and now that they were old she was glad to repay their goodness.

They had put their names down on the council's list for a small home for old people, and Jenny hoped that they would get it, although what would happen to her then, she was not sure. In any case, she told herself, as long as she could work she would be all right. And Jenny was prepared to die in harness.

'No,' she confessed, in response to Winnie's enquiry.

'But, Jenny dear, just because I didn't need anything –'

'I didn't either,' said Jenny, 'but I'll make us both some coffee. How is he?'

'Sitting up and looking better. Did I hear the telephone ring about half an hour ago?'

'Only the exchange people, testing. There was a fault. It's all right again now.'

'That's a blessing,' said Winnie. 'Now as soon as you've had this, Jenny, you must go home.'

'I'll willingly stay. Ma and Pa know how things are here.'

Winnie shook her head.

'You've done more than enough. I don't know how I should have managed without you.'

'Let me know if you want me, Mrs Bailey. I can come back any time.'

'We'll be all right, Jenny, and I'll see you in the morning, anyway.'

She took her cup, and made her way to the door.

'I'll say goodbye now, Jenny. Don't bother to call in before you go.'

'I won't. It might disturb the doctor,' said Jenny.

But when Winnie re-entered the room, she saw that nothing would disturb the doctor again.

He lay back on the pillows, his eyes closed, and his spectacles awry.

The room was very still. Winnie put down the coffee cup noiselessly upon the mantelpiece, and went to look at her husband.

She was surprised to find how calm she felt – as calm as the figure before her. The fear, the panic, the overwhelming sense of loss, which she had so often envisaged, were simply not there, at this moment.

She took the spectacles and folded them neatly, and removed the pen which was still lodged between the thin fingers. She automatically put the fast-cooling hands beneath the bedclothes, and smoothed the rumpled coverlet.

As she did so, she heard the sound of Jenny's bicycle being wheeled to the gate, and was glad to be left alone and in privacy.

She picked up the newspaper which had slipped to the

floor. Still dry-eyed, as if in a trance, Winnie looked at the last entry, and remembered her husband reading out the clue. It was 'Bravery! Many lead the twentieth century', and Donald had filled it in, at the point of death. 'COURAGE' he had written, in faint capitals.

Winnie looked, with unseeing eyes, into the darkening garden.

He had possessed that all his life, and he had fostered it in others, inspiring and strengthening them when most in need.

And now, this one word, his last, might almost be considered as his final message to her.

She sat down by the bedside, and began her silent vigil, as night fell upon Thrush Green.

PART TWO

Fighting Breaks Out

7. *The Rector is Inspired*

On the day after the funeral of the good doctor, Winnie Bailey accompanied her sister when she returned to Cornwall.

The inhabitants of Thrush Green voiced their approval. It was best to get right away for a time, they told each other. The house would be full of memories. Even more distressing, the mound of flowers above the doctor's last resting-place could be clearly seen from the upstairs windows. A very good thing that poor Mrs Bailey should be spared such pain.

The house looked blind and forlorn with all its windows shut. Only the surgery, built at the side, showed signs of life twice a day, when young Doctor Lovell, or his still younger assistant, opened the place from nine till ten-thirty and from six to seven-thirty in the evening.

What would happen to the house now, people wondered? It was a big place for one woman to live in. On the other hand, she had lived there almost all her married life, and she would not want to part with all the loved things around her which she and Donald had shared for so long. It was generally hoped that Winnie would return to Thrush Green, and that the sister would not be able to persuade her to stay in foreign parts.

The quiet weather, which had started on the night of Donald Bailey's death, continued to wrap the countryside in still greyness.

The sky remained overcast, the air humid. The hedges and trees were beaded with drops, and the turf of Thrush Green was spongy with moisture.

Gardeners, anxious to get their autumn digging done, found the heavy Cotswold soil too wet to turn. Lawns waited for their final cutting. Sodden roses, rusty with the damp, awaited pruning, and a general air of lethargy enveloped man and beast.

Tidying the churchyard still went on in a desultory way. The evenings now were too dark to allow much work to be done, but one Saturday afternoon found the rector, Harold Shoosmith and the oldest boy Cooke, from Nidden, busy with bill hooks and shears.

Albert Piggott hovered about ostensibly straightening the vases on various graves, but really watching the intruders on his preserves. That dopey Bobby Cooke, he told himself sourly, didn't know a hawk from a handsaw, let alone a dock from a privet bush. He guessed, correctly as it happened, that his mother had shooed him out of her way. How many was it she'd got? Seven or eight? And she'd been a nice looking girl when they had been at the village school together years ago.

'How's yer mum?' asked Albert, suddenly affable.

'Eh?' said the boy. He wiped a wet nose on the back of his hand.

'How's yer ma?' repeated Albert.

'What?' said the boy. He began to look hunted.

'Lord love old Ireland!' snapped Albert, his brief store of affability vanishing. 'You wants to wash out yer ear-'oles! I asked how yer ma was, that's all.'

'Me ma?' echoed the boy, looking dazed. 'My mum, d'you mean?'

'*Mum, ma, mummy, mother*!' shouted Albert in exasperation. 'Her what bore you – more's the pity! I simply asked – civil – how she was.'

'Oh!' said the boy, and turned back to the hedge again.

Albert, near to gibbering, wrenched at the boy's shoulder.

'Well, answer me then, you dope,' screamed Albert. '*How's yer ma?*'

'All right,' said the boy, looking faintly surprised. He stood there open-mouthed, watching Albert hobble away to a distant vase, muttering the while.

'Loopy!' said the boy aloud, taking a leisurely swing at a lilac bush.

At the further end of the graveyard, Harold and Charles sat on the stub wall and puffed in unison. Their knees were wet and muddied, for they had been crawling along the perimeter path trimming the tussocks of grass which no mower could hope to cut.

'Good of Bobby Cooke to turn up,' commented the rector, putting a hand to his aching back.

'Is it Bobby? I thought that one was Cyril.'

'To be honest,' said the rector, 'I muddle them myself. There are so many Cookes. She used to clean the village school you know, before Nelly Tilling – I mean, Mrs Piggott – did it.'

'Any chance of Mrs P. returning?'

'None, I should say, and in any case I doubt if Miss Watson would want her back at the cleaning – excellent though I believe she was! Your Betty Bell is so satisfactory, I gather.'

'She's a good girl,' agreed Harold.

He caught sight of the eldest Cooke boy slashing at the lilac bush, and hurried to the rescue. The rector rose painfully from his resting place before resuming his task. Certainly the path looked neater, but for how long? And would it be possible to restore the graveyard to its earlier neatness, without at least two men working full-time?

'Sometimes,' he said sadly to his friend, when Harold returned, 'I think we'll have to have those sheep back.

Something drastic must be done. We're only nibbling at it, you know. What we want is a clean sweep.'

Harold nodded.

'Are you free on Monday? I'm running down to Stroud to pick up some rush mats for the kitchen, and I'd like you to come with me, if you can spare the time. There's a graveyard on the way which might give us some ideas.'

'I should like that immensely,' said the rector.

'Right,' said Harold, 'and now back to work. Only another thirty yards to go!'

'Thank God!' said the rector from his heart, sinking to his knees.

Monday was another still grey day, but the mists had lifted, and the distant views showed the autumn fields a patchwork of green, brown and gold.

It was a treat for Charles Henstock to have a day out. His parish duties occupied his time, and as a neighbouring parson was on the sick list, he had been particularly busy helping with his services for the past month.

Harold's car was large and comfortable. What was more, it had an efficient heater which the rector's did not have.

'You should get Reg Bull to look at it,' said Harold, when Charles told him.

'But he has. He services it regularly, you know, and I always mention the heater. I suppose it's beyond human aid.'

'Rubbish!' said Harold robustly. 'Tell Bull you won't pay the bill until the heater's put right. That'll make him move.'

'I really don't think I'm equal to that,' replied the good rector unhappily.

'Then you'll have a cold car. And what's more, so will poor Dimity.'

This was a shrewd thrust, and Charles moved restlessly in his agitation.

'Yes, of course. You are quite right. I must think of Dimity. She's not strong, you know, and with the winter coming on, I suppose I must put some pressure on Reg Bull.'

'Good! You make sure you do. He won't trouble, if you don't.'

Harold navigated a bend in a village street, and drew up by a grass verge. To their left stood a square-towered church of golden stone, set in a large graveyard.

The two men got out and went to the wall which bordered the verge. It was a little more than waist-high, and sprinkled with dots of green moss and orange and grey lichens.

The two rested their arms on the top and gazed before them. Around the other three sides stood tombstones, placed upright just inside the wall. Some were of weathered local stone, some of marble, some of slate or granite, with here and there an iron cross of the late Victorian era.

They made a dignified array, in their muted colours and varied shapes, set so lovingly around the noble church which sheltered them.

The churchyard was a completely flat close-cut lawn. The stripes of a fresh cutting showed how easily a mower could keep the large expanse in order. Only one or two cypress trees, and a cedar of great age, broke the level of the grass, and the whole effect was of space and tranquillity.

'Beautiful!' whispered the rector. 'Simple, peaceful, reverent –'

'And dead easy to keep tidy,' broke in Harold practically. 'We could do the same at Thrush Green.'

'I wonder,' pondered Charles. 'You notice, Harold, that there are no modern graves here. I take it that there is a new burial ground somewhere else in the village?'

'I suppose there is. But I don't see that that should pose a problem. After all, the new addition to Thrush Green's churchyard is quite separate. When was that piece purchased?'

'Just before the war, I believe. They intended to plant a hedge between the old and new graveyards, but war interfered with the work, and in any case, the feeling was that it should all be thrown into one.'

'Would it matter?'

The rector stroked his chin thoughtfully.

'We should have to get a faculty, of course, and I've a feeling that it would be simpler if we only had the old graveyard to deal with as, obviously, they have had here. But I must go into it. I shall find out all I can as soon as we return.'

'So you like the idea?'

'Like it?' cried Charles, his face pink with enthusiasm. 'Like it? Why, I can't wait to get started!'

He threw his arms wide, as though he would embrace the whole beautiful scene before him.

'It's an inspiration, Harold. It's exactly what I needed to give me hope. If it can be done here, then it can be done at Thrush Green. I shall start things moving as soon as I can.'

Harold began to feel some qualms in the face of this precipitate zeal.

'We can't rush things, Charles. We must have some consultations with the village as a whole.'

'Naturally, naturally,' agreed Charles. 'But surely there can be no opposition to such a scheme?'

'I think there's every possibility of opposition.'

The rector's mouth dropped open.

'But if that is so, then I think we must bring the doubters to see this wonderful place. We could hire a coach, couldn't we? It might make a most inspiring outing –'

Harold broke in upon the rector's outpourings.

'Don't go so fast, Charles. We must sound out the parochial

church council first. I must confess that I didn't think you would wax quite so enthusiastic, when I suggested this trip.'

'But why not? It's the obvious answer to our troubles. Even Piggott could keep the grass cut once the graves were levelled. A boy could! Why, even young Cooke could manage that! And we could get rid of those appalling railings at the same time as we put the stones against the wall. It's really all so simple.'

'It may seem so to you, Charles, but I think you may find quite a few battles ahead before you attain a churchyard as peaceful as this.'

Charles turned his back reluctantly upon the scene, and the two men returned to the car.

'You really must have more faith,' scolded the rector gently. 'I can't think of anyone who could have a sound reason for opposing the change.'

'Dotty Harmer might,' said Harold, letting in the clutch. 'And her hungry goats.'

'Oh, Dotty!' exclaimed Charles dismissively. 'Why bring her up?'

'Why indeed?' agreed Harold. 'Keep a look out for a decent pub.'

At that very moment, Dotty Harmer was driving into Lulling High Street.

She was marshalling her thoughts – no easy job at the best of times – but doubly difficult whilst driving. She had a parcel to post and stamps to buy. The corn merchant must be called upon to request that seven pounds of oats and the same of bran be delivered within the next week. And it might be as well to call at the ladies' outfitters to see if their plated lisle stockings had arrived.

After that, she was free to keep her luncheon engagement

with the Misses Lovelock, three silver-haired old sisters whose lavender-and-old-lace exteriors hid unplumbed depths of venom and avarice. Their Georgian house fronted the main street, which gave them an excellent vantage point for noting the activities of the Lulling inhabitants. Any one of the Lovelock sisters could inform you, without hesitation, of any peccadilloes extant in the neighbourhood. Dotty looked forward to her visit.

Halfway along the High Street Dotty stopped, as she had so often done, outside the draper's, and prepared to alight. A short procession of vehicles, which had accumulated behind her slower-moving one, swerved out to pass her, the drivers muttering blasphemies under their breath. Dotty was blissfully unconscious of her unpopularity, and was about to open the door into the pathway of an unwary lorry driver, when a young policeman appeared.

'Can't stop here, ma'am,' he said politely.

'Why not?' demanded Dotty. 'I have before. Besides, I have to call at the draper's.'

'Sorry, ma'am. Double yellow lines.'

'And what, pray, do they signify?'

The young policeman drew in his breath sharply, but otherwise remained unmoved. He had had a spell of duty in the city of Oxford, and dealt daily there with eccentric academics of both sexes. He recognized Dotty as one of the same ilk.

'No parking allowed.'

'Well, it's a great nuisance. I have a luncheon engagement at that house over there.'

'Sorry, ma'am. No waiting here at all. Try the car park behind the Corn Exchange. You can leave it there safely for two or three hours.'

'Very well, very well! I suppose I must do as you say, officer. What's your name?'

'John Darwin. Four-two-four-six-nine-police-constable-stationed-at-Lulling, ma'am.'

'Darwin? Interesting. Any relation to the great Charles?'

'Not so far as I know, ma'am. No Charles'es in our lot.'

He beckoned on a line of traffic, and then bent to address Dotty once more.

'This is just a caution, ma'am. Don't park by yellow lines. Take the car straight to the car park. You'll find it's simpler for everyone.'

'Thank you, Mr Darwin. As a law-abiding citizen I shall obey you without any further delay.'

She let in the clutch, bounded forward, and vanished in a series of jerks and minor explosions round the bend to the car park.

'One born every minute,' said P.C. Darwin to himself.

The luncheon party was a great success. Bertha, Ada and Violet owned many beautiful things, some inherited, some acquired by years of genteel begging from those not well-acquainted with the predatory ladies of Lulling, and a few – a very few – bought over the years.

The meal was served on a fine drum table. The four chairs drawn up to it were of Hepplewhite design with shield backs. The silver gleamed, the linen and lace cloth was like some gigantic snowflake. Nothing could be faulted, except the food. What little there was, was passable. The sad fact was that the parsimonious Misses Lovelock never supplied enough.

Four wafer-thin slices of ham were flanked by four small sausage rolls. The sprig of parsley decorating this dish was delightfully fresh. The salad, which accompanied the meat dish, consisted of a few wisps of mustard and cress, one tomato cut into four, and half a hard-boiled egg chopped small.

For the gluttonous, there was provided another small dish,

of exquisite Meissen, which bore four slices of cold beetroot and four pickled onions.

The paucity of the food did not dismay Dotty in the least. Used as she was to standing in her kitchen with an apple in her hand at lunchtime, the present spread seemed positively lavish.

Ada helped her guest to one slice of ham, one sausage roll and the sprig of parsley, and invited her to help herself from the remaining bounty. Bertha proffered the salad, and Dotty, chatting brightly, helped herself liberally to mustard and cress and two pieces of tomato. Meaning glances flashed between the three sisters, but Dotty was blissfully unaware of any contretemps.

'No, no beetroot or onion, thank you,' she said, waving away the Meissen dish. There was an audible sigh of relief from Bertha.

The ladies, who only boasted five molars between them, ate daintily with their front teeth like four well-bred rabbits, and exchanged snippets of news, mainly of a scurrilous nature.

'I saw the dear vicar and Mr Shoosmith pass along the street this morning. And where were they bound, I wonder? And what was dear Dimity doing?'

'The washing, I should think,' said Dotty, eminently practical. 'And I can't tell you what the men were up to. Parish work, no doubt.'

'Let's hope so,' said Violet in a tone which belied her words. 'But I *thought* I saw a picnic basket on the back seat, with a *bottle* in it.'

'Of course, it's racing today at Cheltenham,' said Ada pensively.

The conversation drifted to the death of Donald Bailey, and even the Misses Lovelock were hard put to it to find any criticism of that dear man. But Winnie's future, of course, occasioned a great deal of pleasurable conjecture, ranging from her leaving Thrush Green to making a second marriage. 'Given the chance!' added Violet.

The second course consisted of what Bertha termed 'a cold shape', made with cornflour, watered milk and not enough sugar. As it had no vestige of colour or flavour, 'a cold shape' seemed a fairly accurate description. Some cold bottled gooseberries, inadequately topped and tailed, accompanied this inspiring dish, of which Dotty ate heartily.

'Never bother with a pudding myself,' she prattled happily, wiping her mouth on a snowy scrap of ancient linen. 'Enjoy it all the more when I'm given it,' she added.

The Misses Lovelock murmured their gratification, and they moved to the drawing-room where the Cona coffee apparatus was beginning to bubble.

What with one thing and another, it was almost a quarter to four before Dotty became conscious of the time.

She leapt to her feet like a startled hare, grabbing her handbag, spectacle case, scarf and gloves which she had strewn about her en route from one room to another.

'I must get home before dark. The chickens, you know, and Ella will be calling for her milk, and Dulcie gets entangled so easily in her chain.'

The ladies made soothing noises as she babbled on, and inserted her skinny arms into the deplorable jacket which Lulling had known for so many years.

Hasty kisses were planted on papery old cheeks, thanks cascaded from Dotty as she struggled with the front door, and descended the four steps to Lulling's pavement.

The three frail figures, waving and smiling, clustered in their doorway watching the figure of their old friend hurrying towards the car park.

'What sweet old things!' commented a woman passing in her car. 'Like something out of *Cranford*.'

Needless to say, she was a stranger to Lulling.

The overcast sky was beginning to darken as Dotty backed cautiously out of the car park and set the nose of the car towards Thrush Green.

The High Street was busier than usual. Housewives were rushing about doing their last-minute shopping. Mothers were meeting young children from school, and older children, yelling with delight at being let out of the class-room, tore up and down the pavements.

Some of them poured from the school gateway as Dotty chugged along. Several were on bicycles. They swerved in and out, turning perilously to shout ribaldries to their friends similarly mounted.

Dotty, still agitated at the thought of so much to do before nightfall, was only partly conscious of the dangers around her. She kept to her usual thirty miles an hour, and held her course steadily.

Unfortunately, one of the young cyclists did not. Heady with freedom, he tacked along on a bicycle too big for him, weaving an erratic course a few yards ahead of Dotty's car.

The inevitable happened. Dotty's nearside wing caught the boy's back wheel. He crashed to the ground, striking the back of his head on the edge of the kerb whilst Dotty drove inexorably over the bicycle.

She stopped more rapidly than she had ever done in her life, and hurried back to the scene. A small crowd had collected in those few seconds, expressing dismay and exchanging advice on the best way to deal with the injured child.

'You take 'is legs. I'll 'old 'is 'ead!' shouted one.

'You'll bust 'is spine,' warned another. 'Leave 'im be.'

'Anyone sent for the ambulance?'

'Where's the police?'

Amidst the hubbub stood the rock-like figure of a stout American boy, known vaguely to Dotty. His face was impassive. His jaws worked rhythmically upon his chewing gum.

He was the first to address Dotty as she arrived, breathless and appalled.

'He's dead, ma!' he said laconically, and then stood back to allow *P.C.* John Darwin 42469, stationed unfortunately – for him – at Lulling, to take charge.

8. Dotty Causes Concern

Ella Bembridge was in her kitchen, her arms immersed in the sink.

She was soaking cane. It had occurred to her, during the week, that she had a large bundle of this material in her shed, and with Christmas not far off she had decided to set to and make a few sturdy articles as a change from the usual ties she manufactured for presents.

This sudden decision had been made whilst examining some flimsy containers in the local craft shop in Lulling High Street. Ella picked up waste-paper baskets, roll baskets, gimcrack bottle holders and the like and was more and more appalled at the standard of work as she took her far from silent perambulation about the display.

'Some are made in Hong Kong,' explained the arty lady in charge, in answer to Ella's protestations.

'So what? As far as I can see, the things from there compare very favourably with this other rubbish.'

The arty lady fingered her long necklace and looked pained.

'There's nothing here that would stand up to a week's use,' proclaimed Ella forthrightly. 'Look at this object! What is it, anyway?'

'It's a hair tidy,' quavered the arty lady.

'A *hair-tidy?*' boomed Ella, much as Lady Bracknell declaimed: '*A handbag?*'

'Who the hell ever uses a *hair tidy?*' demanded Ella. But her victim had fluttered away to attend a less difficult customer choosing joss-sticks, and Ella made her way home determined to look out the cane and fashion something really worthwhile.

The light was fading fast as Ella struggled to immerse the cane completely. She was about to leave it to its own acrobatic writhings and fill the kettle for a cup of tea, when Dimity burst through the back door, wild-eyed.

'Oh, thank goodness you're here!'

'Well, where d'you expect me to be? What's up, Dim?'

'It's Dotty. She's at the police station.'

'That doesn't surprise me. That confounded car, I suppose?'

'Yes, but ... Oh, Ella, it's really serious this time. She's knocked down a boy and he's had to be taken to hospital.'

'That's done it! How badly hurt is he?'

'Someone said he was dying.'

Dimity's eyes filled with tears. Ella, used to her old friend's ways, spoke robustly.

'You know *people*. Some of 'em love a bit of drama. Bet he's only had a bump on the head. Probably been sent home again by now.'

'I hope so. Anyway, Dotty rang up, really to speak to Charles, I think, but he's still out with Harold. She's worried about the animals. They seem to be asking her rather a lot of questions at the police station.'

'Then I hope to goodness she's got her solicitor with her,' said Ella.

'I didn't ask. The thing is, Ella, I'm expecting the men back for tea any minute, and I wondered if you could see to Dotty's chickens and things, before it gets dark?'

'Of course, of course. I'll go straightaway.'

She began to tug at a disreputable anorak hanging on the kitchen door.

'I'll get my milk at the same time. I suppose Dotty'll be back in time to milk Dulcie? That's one job I won't tackle.'

The two friends left the cottage and crossed the road to the green. As they parted, Harold Shoosmith's car drew up, and

Ella heard his cheerful greeting as she hurried off through the dusk to Dotty's hungry family.

The grapevines of Lulling and Thrush Green were at work within minutes of Dotty's accident. She had been born in the little town, and was known to almost everyone in the neighbourhood. The victim too was soon named. He happened to be the third son of Mrs Cooke's large family at Nidden, and he was named Cyril. He was in his first year at Lulling School, having left Miss Watson's care – much to her secret relief – that summer.

Within the hour it was variously known, in Lulling and its environs, that Cyril Cooke was dead, dying, on the danger list, suffering from a fractured skull, concussion, two broken legs, one broken leg, one broken arm, multiple fractures of the pelvis and internal injuries. A few, however, were of the opinion that Cyril Cooke was shamming, and only had slight bruising.

Conjectures about Dotty were equally confused. Some said she would be charged with dangerous driving, careless driving or simply with having no lights. Others said she would face a charge of manslaughter, if Cyril Cooke succumbed to his injuries. There was a certain amount of sympathy for Dotty, but undoubtedly there was also a feeling of 'it-was-only-to-be-expected', laced with considerable excitement at this dramatic turn of events.

It was at Thrush Green that consternation was at its most acute. The good rector was much agitated, torn with anxiety for Dotty and sympathy for Mrs Cooke, whom he proposed to visit at once.

'Who is Dotty's solicitor?' enquired Harold Shoosmith.

'Justin Venables,' answered Dimity. 'Her family has always dealt with that firm. There was a case once against Dotty's father after he had caned a boy. I've an idea Justin handled that case as a young man. Mr Harmer got off, I remember.'

Harold Shoosmith forbore to comment, but was secretly dismayed. He had only met Mr Venables once or twice at social gatherings, and found him a charming old man, silver-haired and gentle. He was also, in Harold's opinion, a good twenty years too old to be practising with efficiency.

'I do so hope that she's had the sense to send for him,' said Charles. 'He's such a wise fellow, and so experienced. This could be a very nasty case, and I wouldn't put it past Dotty to insist on making her own defence. It could be disastrous.'

Harold nodded.

'I take it that one of the junior partners might take it on?'

Charles looked surprised.

'I suppose they might be asked, but I doubt if Justin would let such an old client down. Besides, they're mere boys, mere boys.'

Harold was aware that 'the mere boys' were all around the age of forty, but managed to keep silent. It seemed quite obvious that Dotty would be supported by the aged Mr Venables unless she decided to defend herself. Either course, thought Harold, seemed fraught with danger.

He made his farewells to the Henstocks and set off across the green. It was a pity that such a fruitful day had had to end so disastrously. They had both enjoyed their trip, and certainly Charles now had plenty to think about when planning improvements to Thrush Green's churchyard. Perhaps it was as well, thought Harold philosophically, that he had something else to think of at the moment. His enormous enthusiasm for levelling the graves had quite startled Harold who disliked undertaking anything too precipitately, particularly a project which must certainly face some opposition. By morning, dear old Charles should be seeing matters in perspective, he hoped.

He was shutting his gate, when Joan Young, who was exercising her dog, called across to him.

'You've heard about Dotty's accident, I suppose?'

Harold said that he had.

'Any news of the boy?' he asked.

'Yes. As luck would have it, Ruth's husband was at the hospital, so he examined him. Too early to say yet, the doctor said, but it's mainly head injuries. He's in the intensive care unit.'

'That sounds bad.'

'I feel sorry for that poor Mrs Cooke. She's at the hospital now, I believe.'

'Charles was going to call on her.'

'I'll give him a ring. He can telephone the hospital, and see if she's there. It's poor old Dotty who will need help.'

'I agree.'

'She should never have had that wretched car. We should have seen that she didn't drive it.'

Harold laughed.

'Can you see *anything* we said being considered by Dotty? She's a strong-willed woman – not to say positively pig-headed.'

'True enough,' conceded Joan, and broke into a run as her dog caught sight of Albert Piggott's cat and gave chase.

The morning dawned with a beauty rare in autumn. Fluffy pink clouds reflected the rising sun, and Thrush Green was bathed in rosy light.

After the spell of grey weather it was wonderfully cheering to see the sun again, and prudent housewives made sudden decisions to wash woollies, and gardeners determined to get on with the digging.

At the village school Miss Watson chose: 'Those roseate hues of early dawn have waked me from my sleep,' for the morning hymn, thus confusing several infants, still unable to read, who misheard the opening line and later argued fiercely with Miss Fogerty about 'the rose ate shoes' which needed a lengthy explanation just when Miss Fogerty was trying to fathom the problem of the still-missing emergency knickers. However, infants' teachers are used to coping with such difficulties, and Miss Fogerty was no exception.

The fine weather meant that the children could play outside in comfort, and Miss Watson had time to remark on the sad affair of Miss Harmer's accident.

'I'm afraid I foresaw this sort of thing happening,' she confided to her assistant. There was an element of self-satisfaction in her tone that nettled little Miss Fogerty.

'No one can help an accident,' she responded. 'And you know what boys are on bicycles.'

'My boyfriend,' announced Miss Potter, who should have been on playground duty, but was loitering as usual, 'says that *everyone* should take a test, no matter how long they've had a licence.'

'Has he taken one?' enquired Miss Fogerty, unusually tart.

'Yes, five times,' replied Miss Potter, drifting towards the door.

'That may account for his dictum,' said Miss Fogerty, to the girl's retreating back.

'Have a biscuit, Agnes dear,' said her headmistress hastily. Really, Agnes was getting quite waspish!

'Thank you,' said Miss Fogerty, accepting an Osborne biscuit. 'It ill behoves any of us,' she pronounced in a milder tone, 'to lay blame at *anybody*'s door in a matter like this. I'm sure Miss Harmer and Cyril Cooke both deserve sympathy – not censure.'

'Yes, indeed, Agnes,' agreed Miss Watson, with unaccustomed meekness.

'Bad luck about Miss Harmer, isn't it?' cried Betty Bell when she reported for her morning duties at Harold's. 'I called in to see her on my way up. She don't say much, but she looks a bit shook up.'

'She's bound to be upset,' said Harold diplomatically, watching Betty unwind the cord of the Hoover from the intricate figure of eight which she employed for its resting hours.

Harold had asked her, on many occasions, to wind it straightforwardly up and down, because of breaking the covering of the cord, but he might just as well have addressed the moon on the subject, and was now resigned to the habit.

'She's a funny old party,' announced Betty, dropping the plug with a crack on the kitchen tiles. Harold winced, but remained silent.

'I know she feels bad about that Cooke kid, but she won't say so. Says it was all the child's fault. He wasn't looking where he was going, and she was, and all that. Let's hope she's got some people as'll back her up.'

'There must have been plenty of witnesses at that time of day.'

'Ah, *witnesses*!' agreed Betty knowingly. 'But who's going to *be* a witness? As soon as a policeman comes, they all scarpers, don't they? Don't want to know. Might have to spend a day up the court having questions fired at 'em. You can understand it really.'

'It's a duty, Betty, which every citizen must accept.'

'Well, you try telling that to some of them Lulling lot! The only person I've heard of so far is the butcher. He saw it all evidently. Anyway, Mr Venables'll nobble him, I expect, to speak for old Dot – Miss Harmer, I mean.'

Harold was relieved to hear that the redoubtable Dotty had seen fit to call in help, even if it was in the ageing form of Justin Venables. However, he did not pursue the subject with Betty.

'Thought I'd make a start in the bathroom,' shouted his help, heaving the Hoover towards the stairs. 'You finished up there? Shaving, and that?'

'Yes, thank you,' said Harold. For a moment he felt as he had done at the age of six, when a particularly strict nurse had had charge of him, and demanded to know the most intimate details of his morning sojourn in the bathroom. It was only his advanced age, Harold felt, that kept Betty from just such an inquisition.

Halfway up the stairs she paused and put her face over the banisters.

'Know what I told her? I said them Cookes needed more'n a crack on the head to knock them out. And what's more, it was no good worrying about going to court.

"If it comes, it comes," I told her. "It's no good fretting about right or wrong, or what really happened. It's the chap who lies best wins the case."

She resumed her ascent, leaving Harold to muse on the layman's view of the legal profession.

Surmise and conjecture were thick in the air at Thrush Green all that day, but nobody saw Dotty.

The sun shone warmly, and the inhabitants revelled in this brief span of brightness. Even Dotty's sad affairs could not seem entirely hopeless amidst such sunshine.

The early sunset was as spectacular as the dawn, but in tones of amethyst rather than rose, with a hint of mist rising along the river valley and veiling the ancient Cotswold bridges.

Just before dark fell, a new sign upon Thrush Green

deflected interest from Dotty and focused it upon Dr Bailey's house.

For, against the darkening sky, a plume of smoke rose from Winnie Bailey's sitting-room fire. A few minutes later, Jenny was observed wheeling her bicycle out of the gate on her way home.

Winnie Bailey, the watchers on Thrush Green thought, with immense satisfaction, was coming back!

9. Objections

It was dark when Winnie Bailey arrived alone at her door. She had come from Lulling Station, some two miles away, in the local taxi.

It had seemed odd to travel along the dark High Street. It was months, she realized suddenly, since she had seen Lulling after dark, and its empty streets presented an alien air.

Lights shone from the windows at Thrush Green, and Winnie breathed a sigh of relief as she paid the man. Now, fumbling for her latch key, she heard the sound of the taxi dying away as it ran down the steep hill from Thrush Green.

Inside, the house was so dark that she felt a quiver of fright, instantly suppressed. From now on she must face things alone. Plenty of women came home daily to a dark empty house. She must get used to the idea, she told herself.

She pressed the light switch and made her way to the kitchen. Everything was tidy. Jenny's hand was apparent everywhere – in the dusters drying above the stove, the saucepan with soup in it awaiting heat, the set tray carefully covered with a snowy tea cloth.

Dear Jenny, thought Winnie, warmed by the welcome. She carried her case upstairs, and began to unpack it. A late rose stood on her dressing table. The bed was turned down, and upon investigation, Winnie found a hot water bottle in its midst.

Well, it wasn't so bad coming home after all, thought Winnie, washing her hands. She had been longing to come back for several days, but had dreaded secretly the loss of Donald's presence in the home they had shared for so long.

Jenny's ministrations had softened the blow wonderfully. She could never thank her fully, she realized.

She went downstairs and opened the sitting-room door. Joy flooded through her as she saw the fire. This she had not expected, and the sight of the flames, and the logs stacked in the hearth, made her home-coming suddenly complete.

She paused by the fire, sniffing the scent of woodsmoke, and another indefinable smell which she could not place for a moment, but which disturbed her strangely.

Suddenly, she realized what it was. It was the mingled smell of the eau-de-cologne which Donald always used after shaving, and the faint smell of tobacco. She looked across at the pipe rack where six much-loved stalwarts stood – the cherry wood, the one with the amber stem, the silver banded beauty, and all the others he had loved so well.

The room shimmered through the tears which welled in Winnie's eyes. She had been undone, in one swift moment, by the agonizing poignancy of small familiar things.

She sat down by the fire and let the tears fall. Afterwards, she felt better, and went to the kitchen to prepare her simple meal.

From now on, she told herself as she rubbed her eyes with her damp handkerchief, she would have to put a brave front on things. She was glad to have been alone when grief had overtaken her so completely.

But she was determined that it should not happen again.

She caried her tray to the fireside, breathed in the mingled scents of home, and took up her spoon thankfully.

The sky was clear the next morning when Winnie awoke, much refreshed. To her surprise and relief, she had slept soundly from eleven until eight, and felt stronger for it.

By daylight, the house seemed its usual friendly self, and the dreadful loss of Donald's presence was more bearable.

There were a number of things to attend to. She had a few clothes to wash, some shopping to see to, some telephone calls to make and letters to answer.

She intended to busy herself throughout the day, gradually accustoming herself to the quiet house, without a companion. But as soon as she had finished breakfast she went into the garden.

There were still a few late flowers. One or two roses, their outer petals rusted but still vivid, clung to the bare thorny branches. A few pinks and pansies still bloomed bravely, and the winter jasmine was already putting out its bright yellow stars.

In the shelter of the wall which divided her garden from Tullivers', the Christmas roses were in bud, and Winnie realized, with a shock, that she had made no preparations at all for that festival.

'Hello! Nice to have you back,' said a voice hard by. And there was Phil Hurst smiling at her from the next garden.

'Nice to be back,' responded Winnie. 'Nothing quite like your own home.'

'Are you busy today? Would you like to take your chance and have lunch here? Frank's home for the day.'

'I'd love to. I've got all sorts of things I'm supposed to be doing, but it would be lovely to leave them in the middle and see you both.'

'Right. Do you mind an early meal? Jeremy gets home soon after twelve. Say half past?'

'Perfect,' said Winnie, watching her neighbour speed back into the house where the telephone had started ringing.

She went about her morning tasks, warmed by the encounter, and presented herself at twelve-thirty promptly. A Golden Shower rose nodded about the Hursts' porch, its pale yellow blossoms enhanced by the blue sky beyond. The

November sun was warm upon her back, and a sleek robin bobbed and whistled from the laburnum tree by the gate. Despite the gnawing sorrow which now seemed part of her, Winnie's spirits rose. It was good to be in Thrush Green, good to feel the comfort of sunshine, flowers and birds. Better still, it was good to realize that, no matter how dark the day, 'cheerfulness breaks in'.

She was smiling when the door opened, and Phil greeted her with a hug.

'Hullo! Hullo! Hullo! Hullo!' cried Jeremy, bounding up the hall, and Frank appeared, bottle in hand, to add his welcome.

'I can't tell you how desolate we've felt with the house next door shut up,' said Frank as they lunched. 'Don't ever go away for so long again, Winnie.'

'Somehow,' she said slowly, 'I don't think I shall. You know, Peg was wonderful to me, and her cottage is lovely. We've always been close, right from babyhood, and she's the first person I turn to in trouble. But we couldn't live under the same roof for long. She invited me to, and meant it, but she has so many things to do there – all sorts of clubs and things she helps at, and so many friends – it would have taken years for me to settle there, and I'm sure I should have been in the way sometimes.'

'I doubt it,' said Frank, topping up her glass.

'It's true,' continued Winnie. 'And it's the same with me. My life is here, at Thrush Green. And besides, I couldn't possibly part with three-quarters of my home. Everything in it has some meaning for me – is part of Donald's and my life – it would be like pulling a snail out of its shell.'

'Then it would be a slug,' said Jeremy, passing his plate for more fish in parsley sauce.

'And I don't intend to be one,' replied Winnie, laughing. 'No, we shall visit each other more than we did, and probably spend a few holidays in each other's company, but we each keep our own home.'

'That's good news,' said Phil.

'And now tell me what's been happening while I've been away.'

'The most hair-raising event is Dotty's accident,' said Frank, and went on to tell her what was known.

'And there's also some talk of levelling the churchyard,' said Phil, when Dotty's affairs had been discussed. 'At least, so I gather from Harold.'

'That won't please everybody,' Winnie said. She watched Frank helping to clear the table, and thought what a perfect family scene was here. This was a marriage which had turned out well. The three of them had fallen neatly into place, it seemed with the minimum of adjustment.

When she remembered the girl's unhappy first marriage and the tragedy of her husband's death, she rejoiced that this second venture was turning out so well.

'Time to go back, Jeremy,' said Phil before long. 'Run upstairs and wash. We'll take our coffee into the sitting-room.'

'I wish I could have coffee,' said Jeremy, lingering at the door. 'It's handwork this afternoon and I hate my raffia mat.'

'You shall have a chocolate mint to give you strength,' promised Frank, 'but only when you've washed.'

And the child vanished.

A week or so later, a meeting of the parochial church council took place in the rector's dining-room.

The evening was so cold and windy that even Charles Henstock became conscious that the icy room was not very welcoming, and suggested to Dimity that they should light a fire.

The meeting was at seven-thirty (thus successfully inter-fering with most people's meal arrangements) and the fire was alight by six. Even so, the lofty room was barely warm, despite Dimity's efforts, for the fire had smoked when first lit, and the windows had had to be opened for a time.

Nevertheless, it looked quite cheerful to see a fire in the grate, and when the curtains were drawn and some chrysan-themums set centrally on the table, Dimity was pleased with the result.

If only they could afford some really thick curtains, she thought, fingering the dull green rep ones which she had found at the windows when she came as a bride. These were almost threadbare, badly faded, and completely un-inspiring. The carpet too was equally shabby, but there was no possibility of replacing either curtains or carpet on Charles's modest stipend. Dimity thrust away self-pity, reminded herself of those in worse plight, and went to open the door to the first of the visitors.

It was Percy Hodge from Nidden, who farmed a large acreage north of Thrush Green. His family had been staunch Wesleyans until the present generation, when Percy had fallen out with one of the ministers – for what reason no one could really tell – and had transferred his presence to St Andrew's. As he was very much the head of his household, he was accompanied by his dutiful wife and children, and the presence of the Hodge family at Mattins and Evensong helped to mitigate the sparseness of the congregation.

With him was Mrs Cleary, the widow of James Cleary whose family had run the corn merchants' business in Lul-ling from time immemorial. Hard on their heels came Harold Shoosmith and Miss Watson. She had emerged from the school house just as Harold set off, and they had walked across the green together.

They all exclaimed with pleasure at the sight of the fire,

and Harold thought how much more cheerful the room looked than it usually did. The whole house could do with a fire in every room was his personal opinion, and a sound central heating system as well, but one would need at least twice as much as Charles's salary to afford that, he surmised.

Charles hurried in to greet his friends, and busied himself in setting them round the dining-room table. They left the fire, with some reluctance, as the rest of the council arrived.

'Well now,' began Charles, when they had worked through the usual preliminaries, 'we come to the next item on our agenda: "The Future of the Churchyard". I have a little proposition to put forward.'

He began to expound it with clarity and enthusiasm. The difficulties of its present maintenance and the sadness which the community felt at its dilapidated condition were put forward admirably, and there were murmurs of agreement as the rector made his points.

When he reached the proposal, however, the murmurs grew less noticeable, and Harold Shoosmith saw signs of restlessness among one or two members.

Oblivious of the drop in the temperature of the meeting, Charles described the visit to the churchyard in the west which had done so much to arouse his ambitions for their own.

'The place is an inspiration,' declared the rector. 'And I feel sure that Mr Shoosmith will bear me out.'

Harold nodded.

'It can be done here,' he went on, 'and I don't think there would be any difficulty in getting a faculty.'

He paused and looked hopefully at the faces round the table.

Percy Hodge was the first to speak.

'Mr Chairman, sir, I don't altogether like the idea. This

tampering with graves will upset people. It does me, for that matter.'

'Me too,' said Mrs Cleary, with some indignation. 'My husband and I spent a lot on that cross and kerb for his mother, and now his name is engraved under hers, and I just don't want the stones shifted. Our nearest and dearest are there, in that spot – I may say, that *hallowed* spot – and to have the memorial stones put elsewhere is downright misleading, not to say sacrilegious!'

She was quite pink in the face after this outburst, and poor Charles gazed at her in dismay.

'But they would not be *disturbed*, my dear Mrs Cleary, simply removed to the perimeter of the churchyard. It would all be most reverently done, I assure you. The graves themselves would not be touched.'

'I still think it's wrong,' said Mrs Cleary forcefully, slapping her gloves on the table.

'I must say that I agree,' said Percy Hodge. 'All my family are there from 1796 onward, as near the yew tree as they can cluster, and I'm only sorry there's no room for me, except in the new part. I shall definitely oppose any move to shift the headstones, kerbs and any other memorials.'

Charles's chubby face began to pucker like a hurt child's, and Harold hastily intervened.

'Mr Chairman, I think this is a very natural reaction to the suggestion, and one with which we can sympathize. I'm sure that other parishes who have faced this problem have also had to overcome some misgivings. There is the other proposition, you remember, about the sheep.'

'*Sheep?*' squeaked Miss Watson.

'I can remember sheep in the churchyard,' quavered her elderly neighbour, one of the churchwardens.

'Thank you, thank you,' said Charles. 'It was suggested by someone that if the churchyard stayed as it is now, then a few sheep might graze there and help to keep it tidy.

'That's even worse!' exclaimed Mrs Cleary. 'Sheep indeed!'

'Wouldn't be practical with all the yew there is there now,' said Percy Hodge. 'Fencing alone would cost a small fortune.'

'What about Miss Harmer's goats?' suggested someone, half-jokingly.

Harold saw that Charles was beginning to get distressed as well as dismayed.

'Not goats,' said the rector. 'I don't think either sheep or goats are a good idea myself.'

At this point, Miss Watson spoke up bravely.

'I think the rector's first suggestion is a good one, and we ought to consider it. Those railings are a downright danger, and the state of the churchyard is a positive disgrace. What's the use of my telling the children to keep the place tidy, with that muddle facing them every time they go out on the green?'

'Quite right,' said Harold.

'And to my mind,' continued Miss Watson, 'it's far more irreligious to neglect the dead as we are doing at the moment, than to rearrange things so that the place can be a fitting memorial to those who have gone before us.'

There were murmurs of assent for this point of view, and Charles began to look a little happier.

'That is exactly my feeling,' he said. 'It is quite impossible to get help, either paid or voluntary, to keep the churchyard as it should be. We can put several matters on the one faculty when we apply. The railings should certainly go. The headstones – er, rearranged – and the turf levelled so that a mower can keep the whole space beautifully cut. I do urge you to visit the church which I mentioned. It would be inspiring, I assure you.'

'Know it well,' said Mrs Cleary. 'Looks like a children's playground.'

'I really think,' piped the very old churchwarden tremulously, 'that Miss Watson's point, about the churchyard's untidiness being a bad example for her pupils, is one of the most telling. I should like to see this other place. To my mind, the idea is sound.'

There was general discussion, some against, but more for, the proposal, and the hideous black marble clock on the black marble mantelpiece struck nine before the rector could restore order.

'It seems to me that we should take a vote on this project,' he said at last. 'Those for?'

Eight hands were raised.

'And against?'

Three hands went up.

The rector sighed.

'Later on there will be a notice on the church door. Any objections, I believe, must be sent to the Diocese. Meanwhile, I will find out more about applying for a faculty.

'Thank you, my dear people, a most interesting meeting.'

Mr Hodge and Mrs Cleary were two of the last to leave. Their faces were stern as they shook the rector's proffered hand at the front door.

'You'll see my name among the objectors, sir, I'm afraid,' said Percy.

'And mine *most certainly*,' said Mrs Cleary, sweeping out.

Harold and Charles watched them depart beneath the starry sky.

'Dear, oh dear!' cried the rector. 'Would you have thought it?'

'Yes,' said Harold simply, and began to laugh.

10. Problems at Thrush Green

News of the St Andrew's project soon ousted Dotty's accident as the prime subject of debate at Thrush Green.

As is so often the case, those most vociferous were the people who had the least to do with the church. Several stalwart chapel-goers, whose parents and friends lay peacefully beneath the tussocky grass of the graveyard, were among the first to put their names on the list of objectors to the scheme. Percy Hodge's name, of course, was there, in company with Mrs Cleary's.

'I've been tending the graves of my old grandpa and grandma since I was big enough to hold shears,' Percy said fiercely to Joan Young who had been unfortunate enough to meet him on Thrush Green.

'And then my dad's and mum's. Four graves I've seen to every other week, and four nice green vases I've paid for and put up respectful.'

'It isn't such people as you,' said Joan, in a placatory manner, 'that the changes are being made for. It's dozens of graves that are neglected that make the place such an eyesore.'

'Maybe, maybe! Nevertheless, there's some as adds to the ugliness simply by tending the graves without real taste. Take that one next door to old Mrs Curdle now. I'm not mentioning names –'

Joan Young knew it was a relation of the Cooke family whose grave was under discussion, but let the old man continue.

'– but that woman has put five jam jars along her husband. *Five jam jars*, mark you, and everyone full of dead asters for month after month, not to mention stinking water. Now, there *is* an eyesore! With what she spends in cigarettes she could well afford a nice green vase like mine.'

At 'The Two Pheasants' the debate went on night after night. Albert Piggott, with proprietorial rights, as it were, over the plot in question, found his opinion sought in the most flattering way, and very often a half-pint of beer put into his welcoming hand as well. He had not been so happy since his wife Nelly left him to share life with the oil man.

He adopted a heavily impartial attitude to the subject. He found he did better in the way of *pourboires* by seeing both sides of the question. He saw himself as a mixture of the-Man-on-the-Spot, Guardian-of-Sacred-Ground and One-Still-Longing-to-Work but regretfully laid low by Mr Pedder-Bennet's surgical knife.

'No one who ain't done it,' he maintained, 'can guess how back-breaking that ol' churchyard can be! If I 'ad my strength, I'd be out there now, digging, hoeing, mowing, pruning.'

'Ah! That you would, Piggy-boy,' said one old crone, and the other made appreciative noises of agreement, although every man-jack of them knew that Albert Piggott had skrim-shanked all his life, and that the churchyard had never been kept in such a slovenly fashion until it fell into his hands.

'Well, I call it desecration,' said the landlord, twirling a cloth inside a glass. 'Plain desecration! What, flatten all them mounds containing the bones of our forefathers? It's desecration, that's my opinion. Desecration!'

'I'm with you,' said a small man with a big tankard. 'And not only bones! Take a newish grave now, say, old Bob Bright's, for instance. Why, he hasn't even got to the bones stage! He must –'

Someone broke in.

'Them mounds don't have bones or anything else in 'em!'

'What are they then?'

'Earth, of course. What the coffins displaced. The body has to be a proper depth. That's right, ain't it, Albert?'

Albert drained his glass quickly and put it in a noticeable position on the counter.

'That's right. So many feet, it's all laid down proper, or there'd be trouble. And hard work it is too. Specially in this 'ere clay. But that's what them mounds are, as Tom 'ere says. Simply earth.'

'Another half, Albie?' queried Tom, gratified at being supported by authority.

'I could manage a pint,' said Albert swiftly.

'Right. A pint,' agreed Tom.

'I don't agree about the desecration,' said a large young man with a red and white bobble-hat. 'It's more of a desecration to see it full of weeds and beer cans, to my mind. I'm all for straightening it up. It's the living we've got to think of, not the dead.'

'That's sense!' said the small man who had feared more than bones in the mounds.

'Ah!' agreed Albert. 'It's the living what has to keep it tidy, and the living what passes by and has to look at it.'

He took a long swig at the freshly-drawn pint.

'I'm backing the rector,' said bobble-hat. 'He wouldn't do anything what wasn't right, and I reckon his idea's the best one.'

'A good man, Mr Henstock,' said Albert, wagging his head solemnly. 'Wants to do right by the dead and the living.'

'Well, he's not flattening my Auntie May without a struggle,' announced the landlord, still twirling the glass cloth madly.

'We all respect your feelings,' said bobble-hat, 'but they're misplaced, mate.'

Albert put his empty glass on the counter. It rang hollowly.

'You gotter thoughtful mind,' he said to bobble-hat, with a slight hiccup. 'A thoughtful mind what thinks. I can see that. I'm a thinking man myself, and I recognize a man as thinks. A man as has thoughts, I mean. You understand me?'

'Yes,' said the thoughtful one. 'Want another?'

'Thanks,' said Albert simply.

The lack of harmony among his parishioners affected Charles Henstock deeply. His own enthusiasm for transforming the churchyard had made him unusually blind to the possible reactions of the community.

The fact that there was dissension grieved him sorely. He was essentially a man of peace. Charles had never been called upon to be a militant Christian. Anxious not to hurt people's feelings, uncommonly sweet-tempered and unselfish, it was not surprising that he was generally beloved and, to a large extent, protected from trouble by his well-wishers.

He was quite sure, in his own mind, that it was right to apply for a faculty to alter the lay-out of the churchyard. It was the strife which this decision had aroused which shocked him.

There were other, more practical, worries. The fee for the faculty, if all went smoothly, would be modest enough – a few pounds evidently. But if there were serious opposition, and if legal advice had to be sought, heaven alone knew how much money would be needed! If matters became really desperate, then the whole affair might have to go before a Consistory Court to be fought out. No wonder poor Charles Henstock began to feel that he had put his foot into a hornets' nest. After his initial enthusiasm for the scheme, this fierce opposition from some of his parishioners was doubly shocking.

Dimity watched his unhappiness with much concern. For the first time in their married life he seemed unable to discuss a problem freely with her. It showed, in some measure, how grievously he was hurt by the situation. But to be powerless to help him caused Dimity untold misery.

Thrush Green's rectory, bleak enough at the best of times, seemed more cheerless than ever as the storm winds blew around it.

Storm winds blew in plenty, as it happened, for November gave way to a particularly boisterous December.

Thrush Green, perched on its little hill, caught the full force of the gales which roared across the Cotswolds. A large branch was wrenched from an ancient plum tree in Winnie Bailey's garden. A stone tile was flung from the roof of the Young's house into their greenhouse, and at the village school the lobby door kept up a deafening banging as the infants took their many trips across the playground, and forgot to secure the door as they came and went. If only her class had been housed in the new terrapin, thought Miss Fogerty! If the whole school were disturbed by this endless coming-and-going, well – she was sorry, of course, but it must be expected.

As usual, boisterous weather was matched by boisterous spirits, and the children were restless. Windows rattled, vases blew over, papers were whirled to the floor. Miss Fogerty had difficulty in making herself heard above the din, and the tortoise stove took to belching forth smoke. It was small wonder that the three members of staff were unusually short with each other when they met. The final straw came when Miss Potter, after three days of noisy nose-blowing and sneezing, took to her bed with laryngitis, and her class had to be divided between the remaining two staff. It was at times like these that poor Miss Fogerty counted the years to her retirement, and sometimes doubted if she would ever achieve that longed-for state.

Among the trees at Lulling Woods the wind roared and raged. The last few of the leaves were snatched away, branch clashed against branch, and trunks groaned as they were wrenched this way and that by the elements. And, hard by, at Dotty Harmer's, that indomitable spinster battened down the roof of her hen house, tried in vain to persuade the goats to take shelter, and kept all the animals, wild and domestic, protected from the weather as far as lay in her power.

She was glad to have some extra physical work to do. It saved her from dwelling unduly on the possible outcome of that wretched car accident.

Several weeks had passed since the incident, and still neither Dotty nor Justin Venables yet knew if the police were going to prosecute. Not that Dotty cared unduly if the case did go to court. She had never feared authority – except, perhaps, that exerted by her formidable father – and was quite prepared to face prosecutors, the public of Lulling and the local press, with her usual outspokenness.

No, it was not the publicity which disturbed Dotty. It was the warring factions in her own mind.

On the one hand, she was genuinely distressed to have injured the boy, and his continuing presence in hospital was a constant worry to her. She rang the hospital daily for news of the child, careful not to give her name, for she had a feeling that Justin Venables might not approve of her actions.

On the other hand, she was quite sure that the accident was entirely due to the boy swerving in front of her. Her speed was no more than the thirty miles an hour allowed in

Lulling High Street. She had maintained a steady course, and felt entirely innocent of blame.

But would she be believed? Dotty was fully aware that her eccentricities amused Lulling. Not that she cared a fig what people thought, in the normal way, but when it came to finding witnesses one needed reliable people to back one. Where were they? Among the throng who had gathered round Cyril Cooke and his mangled bicycle that wretched afternoon who, if any, would speak for her?

It was at times like this, thought Dotty, that one could do with a husband, or a really close friend, with whom one could discuss one's fears and doubts. To Ella and Dimity, Winnie Bailey and all the other good friends at Thrush Green, Dotty displayed a calm exterior which belied her inner agitation. Her apparent insouciance worried her friends.

'If that Cooke boy croaks,' said Ella darkly to Dimity, 'I suppose our Dotty could face a charge of manslaughter.'

'Surely not!' cried Dimity, horrified. 'Anyway, wouldn't it be a charge of causing death by dangerous driving?'

'Cooke boys don't croak,' said Winnie Bailey. 'They recover from all the slings and arrows of outrageous fortune. At least, so Donald said.'

'He should know,' agreed Ella. 'He brought most of them into the world.'

'Do you think it would be a good thing to talk to Dotty about it?'

'She evades any mention of it,' said Dimity. 'Charles has tried, and she deliberately turned the conversation.'

'Justin Venables should do that anyway,' pointed out Ella. 'I'm not going to worry poor old Dotty. To my mind, she has some uncomfortable moments despite the good face she's putting on things. With any luck, the police will let the matter drop.'

The only person who truly gauged Dotty's anxiety was Betty Bell, who was rather more perceptive than most of those who dealt with her. She expressed herself on the subject to Harold Shoosmith when she arrived one morning, wind-blown and weather-beaten, to 'have a good bash at the oven'.

Her entry into the kitchen set the hall door vibrating, an upstairs window crashing and a laundry bill, insecurely anchored to the kitchen table, floating floorward.

'Lor!' puffed Betty. 'Knocks all the stuffin' out of you, this wind. Any damage?'

'Only in the garden,' said Harold. 'What about you?'

'It tore my boy's shirt on the line, and I can't find a pair of socks. Blown into Lulling Woods, I shouldn't wonder, and the shed door's bust its top hinge and won't shut. Otherwise we're all right. But I had to give Miss Harmer a hand with the felt on the goats' shed. All flapping loose and them animals eating it as though it's licorice strips.'

'Won't it harm them?'

'Shouldn't think so. They managed an oven cloth and a hank of binder twine last week, and seemed to enjoy them. Funny things, goats.'

'And how is Miss Harmer?'

Betty stood stock still, kitchen knife in hand, and spoke more soberly.

'Worried. Poor old lady! She don't say much, but she's upset about that Cyril Cooke, but won't admit it. She's proud, see. Like she was about driving that car herself. Won't admit she's wrong, ever. I like her for it. Plenty of spunk, old Dot – Miss Harmer, I mean – always had. Stood up to her old father, I've been told, and the only one who could too. He was a Tartar.'

She flung open the oven door and sank to her knees, the better to examine the interior.

'What you been letting boil over then?'

'Stewed apple, I expect,' replied Harold. 'It seemed to spread itself.'

'I'll sort it out,' said Betty, flinging herself to the attack with the kitchen knife. 'And while I'm at it,' she yelled above the din, 'you'd better nip up and shut that banging window before it blows off and down to Lulling.'

Later that morning, leaving Harold's stove spotless and the kitchen in immaculate condition, Betty Bell set off on her bicycle against the strong head wind to return to her home at Lulling Woods.

Outside 'The Two Pheasants' she saw Mrs Cooke waiting for the bus. Two toddlers stood to leeward of their mother, who was looking unusually tearful.

'How's Cyril?' called Betty, dismounting.

'They've sent word to say he's took worse,' said Mrs Cooke, her eyes filling. 'I'm just off to see him. Running a high temperature, so they say. They don't seem to know why.'

'They wouldn't tell you anyway,' said Betty. 'You'll know more when you get there, I expect. You'll feel better when you've seen him,' she added comfortingly. 'Ah! Here comes the bus. Give poor young Cyril my love.'

She watched the three scramble aboard, before turning down the narrow lane which led homeward.

'Poor young Cyril,' she echoed. 'And poor old Dotty too! She's the one I feel sorry for, and that's a fact!'

11. Winnie Bailey's Private Fears

As the end of the Christmas term approached, Thrush Green village school became embroiled in its usual festive arrangements.

Miss Watson's earlier years of teaching had been spent in various large town schools where dramatic talent was fostered by those members of staff who had experience and natural aptitude for the job. Moreover, those schools were equipped with large halls and stages, so that Christmas plays and concerts could be given in comparative ease.

In such sophisticated circumstances had the young Miss Watson developed her enthusiasm for junior drama. It was an enthusiasm which grew with the years, and even led her to the adaptation of children's stories into simple plays, some successful, others decidedly not.

For what Miss Watson seemed incapable of understanding was the simple fact that a crowded classroom, with no raised dais for the actors, no wings in which to wait, no curtains, and certainly no adequate ventilation, is not the place to perform even the most elementary dramatic work.

Consequently, as soon as December appeared on the calendar, poor little Miss Fogerty awaited the spate of suggestions for 'our Christmas fun', knowing full well that all Miss Watson's ideas would be quite impossible to put into operation in the limited confines of Thrush Green school, and quite beyond the comprehension of the un-bookish and inarticulate children who formed the main bulk of the pupils.

'I thought a nativity play would make a nice change this year,' said Miss Watson one morning. 'I wrote a little thing when I was at Aberconway Avenue, and it went down amazingly well, I remember. And only six changes of scenery.'

'But we haven't *got* any scenery,' wailed Miss Fogerty.

'Oh, we can run up something,' murmured Miss Watson vaguely. There was a dreamy stage-struck look in her eyes which turned her assistant quite cold with foreboding.

'I believe the Lulling Operatic Society did "The Desert Song" last season,' went on Miss Watson. 'I should think we might borrow some of their clothes, the head-dresses, and so on, for the three wise kings. And palm trees, perhaps, for the desert scene.'

'There won't be room for the children, let alone palm trees,' said Miss Fogerty tartly, but she was ignored. Miss Watson, when caught in the fever of drama production, became temporarily deaf and blind, as Miss Fogerty was acutely aware.

'My new blue dressing-gown will do splendidly for Mary,' said Miss Watson, 'and I thought I would ask the manager at the Co-op butcher's if we could borrow those two plaster lambs that stand in his windows. They would look very attractive by the manger.'

'There weren't any lambs in the stable,' pointed out Miss Fogerty. 'Only the beasts of the stall, if you remember. Any lambs would be outside, with the shepherds.'

If this crack-brained scheme were to go forward, she thought mutinously, at least let the circumstances be as accurate as possible.

'Then they could stand up-stage in the shepherds' scene,' replied Miss Watson, undaunted. 'I can visualize them, silhouetted against the back-cloth as the dawn slowly rises, turning from black to grey, and then through strengthening shades of pink and gold.'

'We should need to engage a trained lighting team for effects like that,' said Miss Fogerty. 'I doubt if the school fund, which now stands at one pound seventy five – as I well know, as I did the accounts last weekend – could face the bill.'

At that moment Miss Potter appeared.

'I was just discussing the possibility of a nativity play this Christmas,' began her headmistress.

'But we haven't got a stage,' said the young teacher, coming with admirable economy, thought Miss Fogerty, to the nub of the matter.

'We've managed *many times* before,' said Miss Watson, with a touch of frost in her tone. 'And that was when we were less fortunate with space.'

'And where,' asked the girl, 'would this play take place?'

'In your terrapin, dear. The perfect spot!'

And before either teacher could reply, she had drifted back to her own room. Miss Watson had learnt to make her exit at the right moment, if nothing else.

While the rumblings of war were growing ominously in Thrush Green school, Winnie Bailey was engaged in a much more private skirmish in coming to terms with her changed circumstances.

She was lucky, she realized, that her financial situation remained much as it was in Donald's life-time. For many widows, the sudden drop in income was the greatest worry they had to face, and that she was spared, although steeply rising costs, in fuel and rates alone, meant that the old house would be expensive to run. Repairs, too, would be another hazard to face, but the structure was sturdily built and had always been well maintained. With any luck, it should not need much doing to it over the next few years.

The thing was, of course, that it was really too big for one woman. Winnie felt guilty, sometimes, when she read of people crowded into tenements, and thought of her own empty bedrooms.

On the other hand, she loved the house, and could not bear to leave it. Its sheltering walls had enclosed their happy life together. The furniture, the pictures, the loved knick-knacks, all told their story of a lifetime spent together in this small community where both had played useful parts.

No, the house was not the main problem. She intended to stay there, and was willing to retrench in other ways so that she could continue to live in Thrush Green among her friends, and also have room to entertain more distant friends who would be invited to stay.

The worry which most perturbed Winnie, was one of which she was deeply ashamed. She had found, since her return to the house, that she was horribly nervous of being alone in it at night.

She tried to reason with herself about this. After all, she argued, poor Donald could not have protected either of them if burglars had broken in. They never had been so unfortunate as to have intruders, and were unlikely to start now. What would there be, of any value, for a thief to find? There were far more profitable houses to burgle within a stone's throw of her own modest establishment.

But such sweet reasoning did not comfort her. As soon as nightfall arrived, she found herself locking doors, shutting windows, and finding strange solace in being barred and bolted.

She made up her mind never to open the doors after dark to people knocking. Stupid though it might appear, she went upstairs and spoke to them from an upper window. There were far too many accounts in the papers of unsuspecting women who opened doors and were hideously attacked by those waiting. As far as lay in her power, Winnie took precautions against violence.

Nevertheless, her feelings worried her. She tried to analyze them as she took an afternoon walk along the road to Nidden one winter's day. The wind was fresh, and although there was no rain, there were puddles along the length of the chestnut avenue, and water lay in the furrows of the ploughed fields. A pair of partridges whirred across the road in front of her, and Winnie remembered that she had read somewhere that they mated for life. What happened, she wondered, to the survivor of such a devoted couple? Was she too as bereft as she now was?

Things were not too bad during the day. There were so many little jobs to do, and trips into Lulling for shopping when she met friends and had company.

And Jenny, of course, was a constant comfort. She grew to look forward to Jenny's mornings more and more. She was deft and quiet, with the rare gift of speaking only when something needed to be said, but her friendliness warmed the house for Winnie, and the knowledge that Jenny would do anything, at any time, to help her, was wonderfully comforting.

She supposed that she must face the fact that she was run down after the years of nursing and the final shock of Donald's death. She refused to look upon herself as an invalid, but it might be sensible to take a tonic, say, during the coming winter months, and to catch up with the loss of sleep she had so cheerfully endured. With returning strength these unnatural fears might vanish.

It was natural too, she told herself, to feel vulnerable now that Donald had gone. For years now, she had been the protector, taking decisions, fending off unwelcome visitors, sparing Donald all unnecessary cares. It was understandable that there should be some reaction.

She had reached the new housing estate by now, which stretched away to the left, and covered the fields she so well remembered that overlooked Lulling Woods.

The houses were neat and not unpleasing in design, though

to Winnie's eyes they appeared to be built far too close together, and the low wire fences gave no privacy. Washing blew on most garden lines, and a number of toddlers played together in the road, jumping in a big puddle to the detriment of their clothes and their obvious delight.

Winnie smiled at them and walked on.

'Who's that old lady?' asked one of the neighbours, in a shrill treble that carried clearly through the winter air.

Old lady, thought Winnie, with sudden shock! Well, she supposed she was. But how surprising! An old lady, like that ancient crone who lived in the cottage she had just passed, who had a hairy mole on her chin and squinted hideously. Or like Jenny's mother, whose grey head trembled constantly, so that she reminded Winnie of a nodding Chinese doll she had owned as a child.

An old lady, an old lady! The houses were behind her now, and the lane stretched ahead bounded by high bare hedges. On her right stood an empty cottage, fast becoming derelict. She stopped to lean on the stone wall and rest.

The house stood forlorn and shabby, shadowed by a gnarled plum tree. Ivy was growing up its trunk and the recent gales had wrenched some of it from the bark. It waved in the wind, bristly as a centipede's legs.

The garden was overgrown, but the shape of submerged flower beds could still be seen, and the minute spears upthrusting by the house wall showed where there remained a clump of snowdrops.

Behind the house, a rotting clothes line stretched, a forked hazel bough still holding it aloft. Bird droppings whitened a window sill, and from the bottom of the broken front door Winnie saw a mouse scurry for cover in the dead grass by the door step. Neglected, unloved, slowly disintegrating, the house still sheltered life, thought Winnie.

Although no children played, no parent called, no human

being closed and shut the door, yet other creatures lived there. Spiders, beetles, mice and rats, many birds, and bats, no doubt, found refuge here from the cruelty of wind and weather.

It was, she supposed, simply a change of ownership.

She looked kindly upon the old quiet cottage. An old cottage! An old lady! She smiled at the remembrance.

Well, in many ways they were alike. They had once been cherished, had known warmth and love. Now they were lonely and lost. But the house was still of use, still gave comfort and shelter. There was a lesson to be learnt here.

She must look about her again, and try to be useful too. There were so many ways in which she could help, and by doing so she might mitigate the fears which crowded upon her when dusk fell.

It was growing colder. The wintry sun was sinking. The sky was silver-gilt, against which the black trees threw their lacy patterns.

She turned and made her way homeward, feeling much refreshed.

One December morning, Betty Bell set off for her duties at the village school and then at Harold Shoosmith's next door.

The weather had changed, much to everyone's relief. The gales had blown themselves out, and a clear sky had brought frost in the night. Underfoot the grass was crisp with rime, and the remaining puddles were frozen hard.

Betty Bell welcomed the improvement in the weather, and hummed cheerfully as she pedalled along the path to Thrush Green. In front of her, in the bicycle basket, was lodged a large pudding basin which she intended to return to Dotty Harmer as she passed.

Dotty was in the habit of buying enormous lumps of

suet for the birds. The trees in her garden were festooned with it throughout the winter months, and a goodly amount was rendered down into fat. Some of this she mixed with stale bread, oatmeal, currants and chicken corn into a concoction which she called 'my bird-cake', and which was thrust into various receptacles nearer the house for the birds' attention.

Usually there was so much fat that Dotty poured it into a basin, and the resultant dripping went to Betty, who was very glad to have it. It was last week's dripping bowl which was now being returned, with a small jar of tomato chutney of Betty's making, as a little return for the dripping.

She was propping her bicycle against Dotty's hedge when Willie Bond arrived with the post.

'Wotcher, Will. How's auntie?' she enquired.

'All right, but for her back.'

'Shall I take that in for you?'

'Not this time, gal, thanks. It's recorded delivery, see. Got to get her signature.'

'Oh well, you'd best go in first,' said Betty, collecting her bowl, and following her cousin up the path. She went, as she always did, round the house to the back door, as Willie knocked at the front.

She heard them talking, and waited, looking at the chickens who clustered hopefully round her feet, their heads cocked, uttering little hoarse cries of expectation.

Willie's whistling faded away as he went back to his bicycle and Betty rapped on the back door. Dotty, looking even more bemused than ever, opened it.

'Come in. Is it your day, Betty? I must have forgotten.'

'No, it's not,' said Betty. 'I only called in to return the basin. Lovely dripping this time. Must have been beef suet.'

She stopped suddenly. Miss Harmer was looking decidedly queer.

'Here,' said Betty, suddenly solicitous. 'You come and sit down. You look poorly. Had bad news?'

Dotty allowed herself to be propelled towards a kitchen chair. A bad sign, indeed, thought Betty. The letter was still gripped in her hand.

'Had your breakfast yet?' asked Betty.

'No, no. I don't want any.'

'I'll make you a cup of coffee then,' said the girl, pushing the kettle on to the ring. 'I've got a minute or two to spare, and I'll wash up these odds and ends while I'm waiting. This 'ere frying pan can do with a clean. It's all cagged up with grease.'

She set about the job briskly, one eye on the older woman who continued to read the letter.

'Listen to this,' said Dotty, in a stunned manner. '"Dorothy Amelia Russell Harmer drove a motor vehicle on a road called High Street, Lulling, without due care and attention, contrary to Section 3 of the Road Traffic Act 1972." What do you think of that?'

'Nothing!' said Betty stoutly. 'I shouldn't let that put me off my breakfast. You take that letter and all them forms straight up to your nice Mr Venables and he'll look after you.'

The kettle began to rattle its lid, and Betty spooned some instant coffee into the largest cup she could find. She then poured the top of the milk into the steaming brew, and brought it to the table.

'Betty,' said Dotty, 'you've given me the cream, and I always keep that for Mrs Curdle.'

'The cat can go without for once,' replied Betty, unrepentant. 'Your need's greater than hers this morning. Now, I must be off. Soon as you've drunk that, you go up and see Mr Venables at the office.'

Dotty sipped the coffee gratefully.

'It really is delicious with the cream in it,' she admitted.

'You want to take it more often,' advised Betty. 'That cat'll get fatty heart if she has it, and you're not likely to get that – with the little bit you eat.'

She hung up the clean frying pan, stacked the crockery, spread the tea towel to dry, and then made for the door.

'See you tomorrow,' she cried, 'and keep your pecker up.'

She left Dotty folding the grim missive and returning it to its envelope. Pedalling swiftly towards the school, she was seriously concerned about Miss Harmer. Say what you like, it was a shock getting a summons, although it must have been expected. And to think her own cousin Willie brought it to the door!

Poor old Dotty! What with this and Cyril Cooke still on the danger list, the outlook for her was certainly black. Let's hope, she thought, that Mr Venables could help, though, when you came to think of it, he was pretty well as doddery as Dotty. Two for a pair, you might say.

Pushing her bicycle across the playground, Betty gave a rare sigh of despair. Life could be a proper turn-up for the book at times.

12. The Summons

Throughout Lulling and Thrush Green, preparations were in full swing for Christmas.

At Ella Bembridge's cottage, a stack of serviceable waste paper baskets was stacked, flanked by half a dozen stout shopping baskets. Ella was proud of her industry and there was no doubt that the recipients would be pleasantly surprised, being already resigned to appearing delighted with lumpy handwoven ties.

Dimity had washed the figures for the crib in St Andrew's church in preparation for their arrangement. Winnie Bailey was nurturing her Christmas roses ready for the great day, and in all the houses around the green, cakes were being iced, and parcels prepared.

The shops in Lulling High Street were decked with cotton wool, tinsel and bright baubles, and the window of 'The Fuchsia Bush' had a cardboard model of a church, with stained glass windows, illuminated by an electric light bulb in its interior. Flanked, a trifle incongruously, by a lardy cake on one side and a chocolate Christmas log on the other, it still commanded widespread admiration.

The Misses Lovelock, practically next door to the café, were busy sorting out all the unwanted presents, which they had frugally stored away since last Christmas and during the year, for redistribution.

The operation was rather more fraught with anxiety than usual this year, as the list of donors which was scrupulously kept, lest the giver received her own gift back, had been mislaid, and the three ladies were obliged to rely on their failing memories. Acrimony prevailed, as Bertha tried to recall who had presented her with a crinoline-lady tea-cosy, Violet racked her memory in vain for the kind person who had supplied a bottle of 'Dusky Allure', and Ada complicated matters by appropriating anything under discussion for her own pile.

In the dining-room at Tullivers, young Jeremy and his friend Paul Young were busy making Christmas cards. The table was littered with coloured gummed squares destined to be hacked into rough representations of Christmas trees or angels, and a roll of white cartridge paper which put up a vicious fight every time the boys attempted to hold it flat for cutting.

Progress was slow, but their spirits were high and the noise considerable. Half a dozen lop-sided cards, already completed, were propped up on the mantelpiece, destined for mothers, fathers, aunts and uncles.

'And I shall do one for Miss Fogerty,' said Jeremy, snatching up the scissors. 'She'd better have an angel.'

'I shan't waste paper on my teachers,' said Paul roundly.

'Well, I like Miss Fogerty, and she's been sad lately too.'

'Perhaps she's ill,' suggested Paul.

'Having a baby, d'you think?' enquired Jeremy, scissors poised.

Paul, with two years' superiority on the subject, pooh-poohed the idea.

'How can she? You have to be married.'

Jeremy pondered the point.

'Sawny Sam's sister wasn't,' he said, naming the local half-wit. 'She had twins, and she wasn't married.'

'Oh, well,' shrugged Paul, 'twins are different.' He changed the subject swiftly. 'You doing cards for Miss Watson and the new one?'

'No,' replied Jeremy. 'Just Miss Fogerty. I like her best. I hope I don't have to go up next year to Miss Watson's.'

'I heard my mum saying you might come to my school

with me,' volunteered Paul, folding paper with a grubby forefinger.

'Your school?' Jeremy went pink with excitement. 'When? Next term?'

Paul began to wonder if he had let the cat out of the bag.

'Well, it wouldn't be next term, I shouldn't think. Prob'ly next September. That's when the school year starts. Didn't you know you might come?'

'Dad wants me to go away,' replied Jeremy. 'I don't want to, and I don't think mummy does either, but I suppose she has to do what he says. At least, sometimes.'

Paul nodded.

'It's not too bad,' he conceded at last. 'Better than being sent away. You can come home each night and play with your own things. I'd fight for staying here, if I were you.'

'Don't worry,' said his friend, licking a gummed angel and thumping it heavily on the waiting card. 'I'll fight all right, but I want to stay with Miss Fogerty as long as possible.'

He held up the latest card and gazed at it with immense satisfaction.

'Think she'll like it?'

'Smashing!' said Paul.

They continued their labours.

The same subject was being debated by the grown-ups in the next room.

'I can't see any harm,' Frank was saying, 'in going down to look at the place. It doesn't commit us, but if he's due to start next September we'll have to get him entered. Actually, I don't suppose they'll have him until the following year, but we ought to get moving.'

'But Frank, he's so young,' protested Phil. 'And you know how I feel about it. He's getting on perfectly well at the village school, and he has the fun of living at home. What's more, I can see that he is properly fed, and happy. And he is! That's the whole point! Why snatch him from here?'

Frank smiled and shook his head.

'That's partly why. I can see your point, my darling, but don't you see that the very fact that you and Jeremy are so close means that it may not be good for him to stay that way for too long? He's an only child – and likely to be so. You've had to be father and mother to him for most of his life, and he needs the rough and tumble of school to toughen him.'

'He gets the rough and tumble of the village school. He has friends, like Paul next door. Above all, he has a decent home. I can't see why he should be taken away from all that he enjoys, especially after the loss of his father.'

'That's just another reason for getting away to school – away from the unhappy memories he must have when you were left alone. He doesn't say much, but he understands a lot. I think a fresh start, away from Thrush Green, would be an excellent thing for the boy.'

'Well, I don't,' said Phil mutinously. 'And I don't see any point in going to visit your old prep school if I feel that the whole thing is wrong for Jeremy. I hate to say it, Frank, but he is *my* child – mine and John's – and I intend to do what I think is right for him.'

Frank shrugged his shoulders, and walked to the window in silence. Phil realized that she had hurt him deeply and was sorry. Nevertheless, she intended to stick to her guns. She did not mind making sacrifices herself for peace and quiet; but to sacrifice Jeremy's happiness was unthinkable.

'There's no sense in prolonging the argument,' said Frank at last. 'I can see you're adamant, at the moment, anyway. But there's just one last thing I want to tell you.

'If I thought there were any doubt about the school, I'd

give way, but I truthfully was extraordinarily happy there, and so was Robert. The head was a splendid chap – a real inspiration, and he had a fine staff. I know there's been a new head for these last few years, but from all accounts he carries on the good work. Tom, at the office, has both his boys there and they seem to do well. Think about it, my dear. I've Jeremy's welfare as much at heart as you have, and perhaps in a more detached manner.'

At that moment, the telephone rang and he hurried from the room to answer it. It looked, thought Phil, as though he had had the last word on this vexed question, but she knew, only too well, that he had not.

Dotty Harmer had taken Betty's advice on that dark morning when the summons had arrived, and proceeded in her car down the hill to Lulling and up the High Street to the market square where Justin Venables had his office.

She drove with unusual caution, so that the procession of vehicles which she led was of some length, and friends on the pavement had plenty of time to exchange witticisms about Dotty's driving.

Anxious not to offend against the traffic laws in any way, Dotty drove straight to the car park behind the Corn Exchange, as previously advised by P.C. Darwin, and backed carefully between a van labelled 'Lulling Rodent Control' and another bearing the inscription 'Vacuum Chimney Cleansers'.

'And what's wrong with Rat-catcher and Sweep?' muttered Dotty crossly to herself, locking the car.

She then realized that the important envelope was inside on the back seat, unlocked the door, rescued the documents, relocked the door, and decided she should have her umbrella, which necessitated putting the package on the car roof, unlocking the door again, fetching out the umbrella, relocking the door, and setting off. That she had forgotten the package on the roof will surprise no one who has to do these manoeuvres, but luckily Dotty remembered before she had gone far, and only needed to return to collect it before it blew away into oblivion.

Twitter and Venables' office had changed little during the years. Mr Basil Twitter and Mr Harvey Venables, Justin's father, had set up their plate as young men just before the outbreak of World War One, taking over the practice from an eighty-year-old solicitor, and returned to their office at the cessation of hostilities, with honourable war records which rightly impressed the good folk of Lulling and district.

The practice flourished, and with the growth of motor traffic more people needed litigation. A third partner, called Treadgold, was taken on, but was soon discovered to be what Mr Twitter called 'flighty', and when he ran away with the wife of a wealthy land-owner, thus justifying Basil Twitter's misgivings, his name was erased from the board, and Twitter and Venables reigned supreme.

In the twenties, young Justin joined his father in the firm, amidst general approval. 'Very solid chap. Very solid,' was the comment one heard most, and when Basil Twitter succumbed to pneumonia in the wicked winter of 1947, and Harvey Venables to sunstroke in Spain five years later, Justin became senior partner and still so remained.

There were three junior partners, now men in their forties and fifties, but still looked upon, as the rector of Thrush Green had said, as 'mere boys'. The older generation always asked for Justin to attend to their business and were sometimes hurt and suspicious when one of the younger men was assigned to them. Dotty Harmer counted herself lucky to be represented by the senior man at Twitter and Venables.

Justin's office was on the ground floor for the very sensible reasons that, firstly, it always had been, and secondly, the younger men could manage the stairs better.

It was somewhat dark, for across the lower half of the sash window was black gauze bearing the wording 'Twitter and Venables Solicitors' in gold letters, forming a tasteful crescent. The walls were lined with the ginger-coloured matchboarding beloved by the Victorians, and rows of shelves carrying black tin boxes added to the general gloom.

Justin Venables sat behind a massive desk which had once been covered in red leather which had now darkened to brown. Upon it were piles of papers, some tied with pink tape, which Dotty suppposed, correctly, to be 'the red tape' one hears so much about. A hideous cast iron ash tray, bearing the legend 'Long Live Victoria 1837–97' stood at one corner, for the benefit of clients, as Justin did not smoke himself.

A heavy oblong glass inkstand held two cut-glass ink bottles, one containing blue, and the other red, ink. Each was topped by an apple-sized silver lid, and the stand itself was embellished with an engraved silver plate testifying to the fact that it had been presented to Harvey Venables on the happy occasion of his silver wedding. Dotty, not normally observant, could not help thinking that it could do with a polish.

They sat on hard wooden chairs facing each other across the assorted objects on the desk top while Justin read the documents, nodding solemnly.

'You see that you are asked to state if you will be pleading "Guilty" or "Not Guilty".'

'I am *not* guilty,' said Dotty hotly, 'as you well know.'

'Quite, quite,' murmured Justin soothingly. 'A simple clarification at the outset. I think we can fill in these forms together.'

They bent to their task. Justin's beautiful unhurried copperplate filled the appropriate places, while Dotty answered relevant questions and admired progress.

'Well, now,' said Justin, leaning back and looking at his client over his half-glasses. 'We must turn our attention to witnesses. Mr Levy is being most public-spirited, and will add great weight to our defence. It's a good thing his butcher's shop has such a clear view of the scene of the accident.'

'I'm pretty sure,' said Dotty, 'that there was a school teacher near the playground gate. He might help.'

Justin made a note on a little pad.

'And some boys, of course,' added Dotty.

'Boys are sometimes unreliable,' said Justin weightily.

'Perhaps some of the other shopkeepers might have seen something,' said Dotty hopefully.

'Maybe, maybe,' agreed Justin. He leant back again and put the tips of his fingers together. He blew thoughtfully upon them for a minute.

Outside, Dotty could hear a dog barking, and the raucous squabbling of the starlings which lived in the eaves of Twitter and Venables' property. Two women talked and laughed together, and Dotty thought how lucky they were to be there in the normal bustle of the street, and not cloistered in this fusty room with all the cares of Christendom which she was bearing.

She sighed involuntarily, and Justin put on his professional air of modified hope.

'Now, don't be cast down, Miss Harmer. We have a very good case, you know. I have every confidence that we shall be successful. I shall make it my business to get in touch with Mr Levy at once, and no doubt he will know other reliable witnesses. It is a pity, of course, that you were alone in the car. A passenger could have been of vital importance. Vital!'

'I don't propose to carry a passenger in my car in the expectation of an accident,' said Dotty bridling.

'Quite, quite,' said Justin. He patted the papers together, and stood up.

'I really think that is all that we can do at the moment, but I shall be in touch, naturally, at every step. I see we have a month before we need to appear at court. Much may happen, I assure you, Miss Harmer. We must live in hope, live in hope.'

He accompanied her to the front door, and watched her cross the market square. The hem of her coat had become unstitched, he noticed, and her stockings were in wrinkles round her skinny ankles. Really, she dressed in a deplorable manner.

It was a great pity, he thought, returning to the office, that he could not ask her to dress decently for her court appearance. It could make all the difference.

But there it was. One must take the rough with the smooth in this life!

He rang his bell, and Miss Giles, who had been with the firm for almost as long as Justin had, appeared at the door with a cup of coffee.

'Mr Baxter from the car dealer's is waiting, Mr Justin,' she said.

The rough with the smooth, thought Justin! After Dotty, Mr Baxter would be very smooth indeed.

'Show him in,' said Justin, 'and bring another cup, if you please.'

13. A Question of Schools

When Dotty heard from the sister in charge that Cyril Cooke 'had had a slight set-back', she found herself trembling as she replaced the receiver.

'A slight setback!' Unspecified, of course, but it could mean anything from bed sores to a serious relapse. All that she had elicited so far had been such euphemisms as: 'Comfortable' or 'Making progress' or 'Getting on quite nicely' which, though vague in the extreme, were mildly reassuring. 'A slight setback' sounded ominous.

She muddled about her domestic affairs in her usual haphazard way, her mind much agitated. After lunch, taken standing, with a stalk of celery in one hand and a lump of cheese in the other, she could bear it no longer, and decided to call on Mrs Cooke.

That lady was taking some dilapidated tea cloths from the line when Dotty arrived, and took her visitor to the shelter of the back porch, but did not invite her inside. To Dotty this appeared a bad sign.

She had called on Mrs Cooke once or twice since the accident, and although somewhat truculent, Cyril's mother had not been actively hostile. This afternoon, however, she looked decidedly grim.

'I came for news of Cyril,' said Dotty coming straight to the point. 'The hospital people said that he had had a slight set back.'

'You can say that again,' said Mrs Cooke menacingly. 'I saw that poor child, after they'd sent word he was bad – and bad he is! High temperature, tossin' and turnin', and can't swallow nothin'.'

'I am very sorry to hear it,' said Dotty.

An ugly flush crept up Mrs Cooke's grimy neck and over her face.

'Yes, you should be too. See where your rotten driving's landed my poor boy! If he passes on, his death'll be laid at your door. And rightly too.'

Dotty, inwardly shaken, nevertheless held her ground. She had faced worse than this in her father's time.

'I am not going to argue with you, Mrs Cooke, about a matter which must be decided in court. I simply came to see if there was any practical way in which I could help, and to find out the latest news of the boy.'

Mrs Cooke suddenly lost control.

'You clear off! Go on, clear off! I've enough to put up with, worrying about my boy what you've near enough done in! You old maids don't know what us mothers suffer!'

She advanced upon Dotty with upraised fist. A lesser woman would have fled in the face of such threats. Dotty stood stock still. Her steady gaze was fixed upon Mrs Cooke's inflamed countenance.

Despite her raggle-taggle appearance, there was dignity in Dotty's demeanour, her back straight as a ramrod, her face expressing cold disdain.

Mrs Cooke stopped in her tracks, and let the intimidating arm fall to her side.

'I can sympathize with your concern,' said Dotty, 'but I deplore your insulting behaviour. I shall bid you good day.'

She turned and strode towards the gate, watched by Mrs Cooke. It might have been her father all over again, thought that lady, and everyone knew what he was!

'Murderess!' she shouted after her.

Dotty returned in good order outwardly, but was seriously upset by the turn of events. Her anxiety for the boy's condition was now tempered with concern for her own position if the child succumbed. This possibility had never really occurred to her, and Mrs Cooke's final dreadful word rang in her head.

Of course, it could never be construed as murder! There would have to be intent, surely, plotting or passion or some true evil, thought Dotty, clinging to those principles with which she was familiar. But it could well be a charge of causing death by dangerous driving, she supposed. Should she call on Justin Venables and find out? What an appalling thing!

Dotty was not normally imaginative, but anxiety thrust a hundred horrid scenes into her agitated mind. She could see herself in one of those dreadful cells, at Holloway, wasn't it? The window always appeared to be hermetically sealed, in the pictures she had seen of the place, and the very thought produced acute claustrophobia. And to hear a key being turned in the lock, and to know that one could not possibly get out! Naturally, prisons had to be secure, that was sensible, but it did not lessen their terror.

Then the food, she had heard, was so starchy, most unhealthy, and the company would, at best, be suspect. Dear, oh dear, what a prospect! And for how long, she wondered?

And who, she thought with sudden shock, would look after the animals while she 'did time', if that was the right expression? This last terrible thought stabbed her to the quick. Would Ella, perhaps, of her charity, see that they were fed and cared for? It was a lot to ask, and one could not really expect such kindness if one were a common criminal.

A common criminal! Something about the cold phrase acted like a splash of icy water upon the fever of her imaginings.

She was *not* a common criminal. She was an unhappy woman who had, by sheer accident, knocked down a boy who had crossed her path. She was in the right. She must hang on to that basic fact. Dear Justin had been hopeful, and she would be too. For had not her upright father said many times that if one spoke the truth and shamed the Devil then right must prevail?

She turned into her gate slightly comforted, and set about preparing the animals' last meal of the day.

That the goats received the chicken's mash, and the chickens received the goats' cabbages was some small indication of Dotty's inner turmoil. Not that they complained. Dotty's charges soon learnt to be adaptable, and to be grateful for favours received.

One winter evening, Charles Henstock paid a call upon his friend Harold Shoosmith.

It was clear and cold. The stars were already pricking the sky, and frost was in the air.

Charles was glad to settle by Harold's log fire, and to accept a small whisky and water.

He looked about the room appreciatively. There was a fine cyclamen on the side table, leather-bound books on the shelves, and a well-filled tantalus on the sideboard. Everywhere the hand of Betty Bell was apparent in the glossy furniture, the plump cushions, the shining glass.

'You manage to make things so very comfortable,' commented Charles. There was a wondering note in his voice. 'Somehow the rectory never achieves such snugness.'

Harold could hardly point out that good curtains and carpets were one of the basic requirements for soft living, and an ample income another, to supply other amenities, including first-rate domestic help.

'I have the advantage of lower ceilings, for one thing,' said Harold, 'and not such an exposed position. Those Victorian Gothic buildings never were designed for cosiness.'

'Dimity does wonders,' went on Charles, nursing his

glass. 'When I think how bleak the house was when I lived there alone, I never cease to be thankful for her presence. Do you remember Mrs Butler who kept house for me?'

'I shall never forget her,' said Harold firmly. 'I have never, in all my travels, met a meaner, tighter-fisted old harridan.'

Charles looked shocked.

'Oh, I wouldn't say that,' he protested.

'Of course you wouldn't. But it's true. I remember the disgraceful way she allowed you to be neglected when you had flu, only bringing up a water biscuit or two when she deigned to climb the stairs! You were sorely put upon, you know that, Charles. Saints often are.'

'She was rather *frugal*,' admitted the rector. 'But why I mentioned her was that I heard by chance that she has married again.'

'Poor devil,' said Harold. 'I hope he belongs to a good club.'

'I really came,' said Charles, changing the subject tactfully, 'to have a word with you about this matter of the faculty. So far there are eight names on the list of objectors, but I fear that there may be some who object in their hearts but have not the courage to state so publicly.'

'In that case,' said Harold reasonably, 'they shouldn't worry you. I suppose you still want to go ahead and apply?'

'I do indeed. And so, of course, do most of the parochial church council members, as you know.'

'I believe we could get the churchyard taken over by the parish council, if that body were willing. It has been done elsewhere, and then of course the upkeep comes out of public funds.'

The rector put down his glass with a quick gesture of repugnance.

'I shouldn't dream of it,' he said sharply. 'Would you?'

'No, indeed. I think it is the church's business and should remain its responsibility.'

'Absolutely! Absolutely!'

'I only mentioned it as a way of solving our problem. Somehow, I didn't think you would jump at the idea.'

'My chief worry is two-fold,' said Charles. 'The village must agree about the matter, so that there are no grievances, and secondly, we must consider expense.'

'The faculty shouldn't run us into much more than ten pounds or so,' said Harold. 'The church funds can stand that all right.'

'I'm aware of that. What disturbs me is the possibility of a real battle in the village. If those eight objectors are truly all we have to contend with, then there's hope. But if, suddenly, more join the fight, we may even need to call in lawyers, and you know what that means!'

'It won't come to that.'

'Who can tell? I was talking to the vicar of my old parish at the Diocesan Synod last week, and their affair went to a hearing in the Consistory Court. The expense was astronomical. It depressed me very much.'

Harold took his friend's glass to the sideboard to replenish it.

'I still say, it won't come to that. We'll fight our own battle here at Thrush Green. I feel sure that we can talk to the objectors on their home ground, and get them – or some of them, anyway – to see things as we do.'

'You won't get Percy Hodge to,' said Charles, accepting the glass. 'He hasn't appeared in church since the meeting, and I fear that he is deeply hurt. The graves of his forefathers mean a great deal to him. It makes me very unhappy to see such bitterness.'

The rector sighed.

'Ah well, Harold. It does me good to talk over things with

you. Somehow, they are never quite so bad after a gossip in this cheerful room.'

He prodded a log with the toe of a shabby shoe.

'Do you pay much for logs?' he enquired.

Harold told him.

'And how much is coal?'

Harold told him that too.

Charles looked thoughtful.

'Perhaps that's why we so seldom have a *big* fire,' he said, quite without self-pity. 'Dimity deals with the bills to save me trouble, and so I hadn't quite realized how much a *big* fire costs.'

He stood up and smiled radiantly.

'But how lovely it is,' he cried. 'I can quite understand people practising fire worship. I'm a little that way myself, I believe!'

The night air was sharp as he crossed the green. Already the grass was becoming crisp with frost. Two miles away, at Lulling Station, a train hooted, and from Lulling Woods, in the valley on his right, an owl quavered and was answered by another.

His tall house loomed over him as he unlocked the front door. It looked gaunt and inhospitable, he realized. His thoughts turned on the conversation he had just had with Harold.

He found Dimity in the sitting-room, close to the fire. It was half the size of the one he had just left, he noticed, un-usually observant. One could see the edges of the iron basket which held the fire. The coals were burning only in the centre of the container.

He looked aloft at the distant ceiling, and at the expanse of sparsely curtained window space. Although the night was still, some wayward draught stirred the light drapings.

The lamp by which Dimity was seated had a plain white

shade which threw a cold light upon the knitting in her hands. Harold's shades, he remembered, were red, and made a cheerful glow.

'My dear,' he said abruptly. 'Are you cold?'

Dimity looked surprised. She put down her knitting, the better to study her husband.

'Why no! But you must be. Come by the fire.'

He threw off his coat and took the armchair opposite her, spreading his hands to the meagre warmth.

'I don't mean just now, my dear. Do you find the house cold? Habitually, I mean? Do you find it colder, say, than Ella's?'

'Much colder,' agreed Dimity, still looking puzzled. 'But naturally it would be. It faces north, and it's twice the size.'

'And we don't heat it as well, I fear,' said Charles.

'Ella always liked more heat than I did.'

'I've just come from Harold's. His fire seems enormous. I'm beginning to think we must give a very chilly welcome to visitors here. But my main concern is for you. You know that you tend to be bronchial. We really must keep a better fire, or see if we can put in some central heating of some sort.'

'Charles dear,' said Dimity, 'it simply can't be done. Do you know how much coal costs?'

'Harold told me. I couldn't help thinking that he must have made a mistake. Why, as a boy, I remember coal carts coming to the house with a large ticket displayed, saying two-and-six a hundredweight.'

'And that,' pointed out Dimity, 'was over half a century ago! Times have changed, and I'm sorry to say that Harold's figure is the correct one.'

'There must be many ways of making this place snugger,' argued Charles, looking about him with fresh eyes. 'What about a red lamp shade, like Harold's?'

'We could do that,' said Dimity, nodding.

'And a screen? My mother had a screen. She said it kept off draughts. And a sausage filled with sand at the bottom of the door. That would help.'

Dimity suddenly burst into laughter.

'Oh Charles! To see you as a domestic adviser is so funny! And such a change! What this house really wants is double-glazing, central heating, thick curtains and carpets, cellars stuffed with coal, and a log shed filled with nice dry logs. But we should need to find a crock of gold, my dear, to provide ourselves with all that.'

'But the shade,' pleaded Charles. 'And the screen?'

'We'll manage that, I think,' smiled Dimity. 'And I'll make the door sausage before the week is out. By the way, its proper name is a draught-excluder.'

'Let's hope it lives up to it,' said Charles, recklessly putting two lumps of coal on the fire.

The subject still occupied Charles's mind later that night. Beside him, Dimity slept peacefully, but the rector could not rest.

There was no doubt about it, he was failing as a husband if he could not provide such basic things as warmth and shelter for his wife. It was not fair to expect Dimity to put up with such discomfort. He was used to it. He hardly noticed it, unless it was drawn to his attention, as it had been that evening, by the contrast between Harold's circumstances and their own.

Well, he supposed that he could look out for another, better-paid, living; but the thought appalled him. He loved Thrush Green, and now that he had embarked on the church-yard venture it would seem cowardly to run away from it and all its many problems.

Then there was the possibility of part-time teaching at the prep school in Lulling which Paul Young attended. Charles was friendly with the headmaster, and he recalled now that only a week or two earlier he was saying that he was looking out for someone to take Religious Instruction. No doubt, he had been sounding him out, thought Charles, but at the time he had not realized that, in his innocence.

But would it bring in any reasonable sum? And how much of that would be taken away in tax? And had he really the time to pay three or four visits a week to the school? His parish was an extensive one, and he took sick-visiting seriously. It was one of the qualities which endeared him to his flock.

The poor rector tossed unhappily. Something must be done. He had certainly been failing in his duty towards Dimity. Because she was so uncomplaining, he had let things slide.

'Sins of omission!' sighed Charles, thumping his pillow. 'Sins of omission! They must be rectified.'

He fell asleep soon after three o'clock, and dreamt that he was stuffing a red draught-excluder with sausage meat.

14. Dotty's Despair

As the end of term approached, the preparations for the nativity play made uneasy progress.

Miss Watson turned a blind eye and a deaf ear to the protests of her truculent staff, but some points had to be conceded.

For one thing, Miss Fogerty refused point blank to try to train the infants in speaking parts. They were too young for it. They would be unreliable and let the others down. They could sing the carols at the end of the performance and she was quite willing for them to take non-speaking parts, such as oxen and asses and so forth, which were well within their capabilities, but the speaking cast must come from the junior school.

When little Miss Fogerty adopted this militant attitude, Miss Watson knew that she must give way. Dear Agnes was usually so cooperative, but there was no doubt about it, she had not been her usual tranquil self this term, and it would be as well to humour her.

Consequently, the long desk at the side of the infants' room was piled high with animal masks of extraordinary variety. The most life-like was one made by an artistic young mother who had adapted an oblong box, which had once held sticks of chalk, into a splendid muzzle for a cow. With a head-dress of magnificent horns, her daughter was the envy of the class.

There were several donkeys, recognizable mainly from their long ears, although most of them drooped so pathetically that Miss Fogerty privately thought that they looked more like the Flopsy Bunnies. However, the mothers would form the most important section of the audience, and the eyes of these beholders would see only beauty and delight.

To Miss Watson's secret dismay, Miss Potter was being extremely awkward about using the terrapin hut for the performance. She ignored her headmistress's requests to take down models, remove sand trays, dismantle the nature table and generally clear away such obstacles which would impede rehearsals. She also refused point-blank to attempt to make scenery of any sort. Miss Watson was nonplussed by this rebellious attitude.

'No one has scenery now,' the girl assured her. 'If we must have this play which, frankly, I think far too ambitious for these children, then the audience must imagine the settings. We were always taught at college that it was better training for the children to leave the stage clear for their own interpretations. Besides, where could we store the stuff? And who's to assemble it and take it down?'

There was much good sense in these remarks, but Miss Watson could not get over the fact that they had been expressed by a very junior member of staff to her headmistress. To give up the idea of the play was out of the question. Nevertheless, if it were to be done at all, it would have to be done, as Miss Potter said, without scenery.

'We've always managed before,' Miss Watson told her frostily, 'but there's no harm, of course, in making the experiment. Let no one say that I set my face against progress! We'll try it without scenery. It will certainly simplify matters.'

Miss Potter's partial victory, however, did not seem to sweeten her attitude to the project. Her children were slow to learn their lines, their costumes were slipshod, their movements ungainly. Miss Watson's and Miss Fogerty's classes were well-trained and showed up the deficiencies of the younger juniors. Miss Watson found it all very vexing. In the old days she could have discussed the difficulties with

Miss Fogerty, but that lady's distant manner did not encourage confidences.

It was a wretched time for all concerned, and when the great day came, Miss Watson was obliged to go into the terrapin herself to take down pictures, diagrams and wall charts which she had expressly asked Miss Potter to remove. One would have thought the girl would have realized that the Three Wise Men would not look right against a background of 'Wild Birds of Britain' and 'Have You Learnt Your Kerb Drill?' Or was she being deliberately obstructive?

Torrential rain persisted throughout the day, so that the cast were obliged to wear wellingtons under their Eastern costumes, and the dark powder ran in rivulets down their faces as they splashed from the school to the terrapin. Matters were not improved by Miss Potter asking audibly what could you expect without a green room at the terrapin?

By the time the mothers and their young children arrived, the playground was awash, and still the rain fell. The lobbies were cluttered with dripping prams and umbrellas, and steam rose from the audience when at last they had paddled through the floods to their uncomfortable seats. Miss Potter and Miss Fogerty wore looks as black as the clouds above whilst trying to keep their flocks in order.

It says much for Miss Watson's self-control that she was able to welcome her packed audience with smiles, and to assure them of 'a lovely performance'.

Before the clapping had died down, one of the Flopsy Bunnies was led on by Joseph, horribly impeded by a blanket which had slipped from his shoulder, and followed by Mary in Miss Watson's blue dressing-gown which, she was sorry to see, was trailing along the wet floor, much to its detriment.

There was a painful silence, broken only by the thumping of Joseph's walking stick on the boards and the impatient prompting by Miss Potter from her seat on the side radiator.

At last Joseph gave tongue and Thrush Green's ill-fated nativity play stumbled into life.

Apart from one disastrous incident in the shepherds' scene, when young Richard Wright found himself pinned to the floor by the heavy foot of a Flopsy Bunny, and was unable to rise after his obeisances, and consequently uttered a terrible word which should have been unknown to, let alone uttered by, one of such tender years, all went well.

Miss Watson and Miss Fogerty turned pink. Miss Potter shrugged her shoulders. The mothers tried to suppress their giggles, and the play continued. But no one could pretend that it was a success, and when at last the children bowed, Miss Watson had the uneasy feeling that the applause was of relief rather than rapture.

When the last of the mothers and children had splashed homeward, Miss Watson surveyed the general chaos of chairs, muddy floor, and discarded costumes.

'Well,' she said, with forced brightness, 'it went better than I expected.'

Miss Fogerty preserved an ominous silence.

'I thought it was a disaster,' said Miss Potter shortly. She took her coat from the peg on the door, and set off for home, with never a backward look at her ruined classroom.

Winnie Bailey observed the exodus of mothers and children from her bedroom window. She had gone upstairs to put on her coat, ready to make a dash through the rain to St Andrew's church.

How dark it was! How wet and gloomy! But there, she told herself, it would be the shortest day very soon, so what could you expect? She had been kept in by the appalling weather, all that day, and felt that she must have a breath of air before settling by the fire for the evening.

She had promised to be responsible for the Christmas

roses on the altar on Christmas day. Were there any pin holders in the vestry cupboard, she wondered? It was a good excuse for an airing. Tying a scarf over her head, Winnie set out.

Rain lashed her umbrella, and the onslaught took her breath away. She was glad to gain the shelter of the church porch. Across the road, she saw Albert Piggott's morose countenance pressed against the window pane. He was keeping a sharp eye on his property evidently, thought Winnie, shaking her umbrella free from drops.

She pushed open the door, and was met by that indefinable smell of damp stone, hymn books and brass polish which greets so many church-goers. She made her way to the vestry, which stood below the belfry, and began to rummage in the cupboard which held vases, crumpled chicken wire, balls of plasticine and other aids to flower arranging. At the very back of the bottom shelf she found four pin holders, heavy and prickly. Should she take them home for safety, or should she leave them here and trust that none of the other flower ladies appropriated them?

She had just decided to take two and to leave two, when she heard a faint noise. Tip-toeing to the door of the vestry she gazed down the length of the aisle. A small figure was kneeling in one of the front pews.

It was so dark by now that Winnie could not recognize the person, although she guessed it was a woman. She hoped that her movements had not disturbed whoever-it-was at her devotions.

She tip-toed back to the cupboard and replaced two of the pin holders. The remaining two she thrust into her handbag.

Very quietly she emerged from the vestry and began to tip-toe to the door. At that moment, a loud sniff shattered the silence. The little figure stumbled from the pew and hastened up the aisle towards Winnie, who saw, with astonishment, that it was Dotty Harmer, and that she had been weeping.

Winnie did not speak until they were both in the porch. She retrieved her umbrella.

'I'm going back, Dotty dear, to make myself some tea. Come and join me.'

Dotty nodded.

Winnie put up the umbrella, and linked Dotty's frail arm into her own. The lights were beginning to glow from the windows at Thrush Green.

'Not fit to be out,' shouted Winnie above the noise of the wind and rain. A faint pressure on her arm showed that Dotty had heard, but she said nothing. Winnie began to find this unusual silence unnerving, and was glad when they reached her home and she could busy herself with the latch key.

'Come by the fire, Dotty, while I put on the kettle. Here, let me take your mackintosh. It can drip in the kitchen.'

She drew a chair close to the blaze and settled the woebegone figure in it. There were no tears now, but Dotty looked white and exhausted. What could be the matter?

When she returned with the tea tray and a plate of home-made shortbread, she found Dotty leaning back with her eyes closed, but to her relief she sat up when Winnie began to pour the tea, and drank the liquid as though she had not had food for hours.

'That *was* good, Winnie dear,' she said thankfully, replacing her empty cup. 'I don't usually bother with tea.'

'Did you bother with lunch today?' asked Winnie, emboldened by the improvement in her guest's condition.

'Well, no. To tell the truth, I was a little upset yesterday, and didn't sleep last night.'

She stopped, took off her glasses and began to polish them

with the hem of her petticoat. Without her spectacles, Winnie noticed, her face seemed very small and vulnerable. A short-sighted child might look like that, bewildered and questioning.

Winnie said nothing. She was determined not to pry into Dotty's troubles. She knew about the impending court case and suspected that this breakdown might have something to do with it. But somehow, it was not in keeping with Dotty's habitual chirpiness. She had given no sign, over the last few weeks, of caring deeply about the affair. It was odd that she should collapse now.

Dotty accepted her second cup of tea and stirred it slowly, her eyes on the dancing flames.

'I went to see Mrs Cooke yesterday,' she began. 'At Nidden, you know. The mother of the child who swerved in front of my car.'

'I know,' said Winnie.

Dotty put down her cup, and began to tell Winnie the whole appalling tale. The anxiety, the daily bulletins, the horror of the child's relapse, the possibility of the boy dying, of taking another's life – it all poured out, until the dreadful climax was reached of Mrs Cooke's blood-chilling cry of 'Murderess!' which had haunted poor Dotty ever since.

'And so you see why I was in church, Winnie. I simply had to tell someone. Someone I could trust. Living alone does tend to make one exaggerate one's fears and I couldn't stay in the house a moment longer.'

'You did the right thing,' Winnie assured her. Dotty's fingers were pulling her handkerchief this way and that in her agitation.

'And now I've burdened you with it,' cried Dotty distractedly. 'You won't ever tell anyone, will you, Winnie dear? I couldn't bear Thrush Green to get wind of my shameful fears.'

'No one will learn anything from me,' Winnie promised. 'And you know, Dotty, we all have fears, and I'm beginning to realize that we must accept them and not feel ashamed of them.'

She went on to tell Dotty about her own nervousness at night-time in the house, and how difficult it seemed to overcome it. As she spoke, she noticed that the handkerchief was put away, that Dotty was nodding agreement, and drinking the second cup of tea, engrossed in someone else's troubles now.

'Perhaps I could come and sleep here,' said Dotty eventually, 'at least for a bit, until you feel better about things.'

'I shouldn't dream of allowing you to,' said Winnie. 'If you can cope alone, down at Lulling Woods, which is far more remote than this place, then I can too. I shall get used to it in time, but what I'm trying to say, Dotty, is that it does no good to torture oneself with guilt and shame simply because one has fears. We're *right* to have fears about some things; evil, for instance, and violence and lying, and I'm not going to add to my misery by feeling ashamed of my loneliness. I am lonely now, but it will pass. You are desolated now by what might occur, but that will pass too.'

Dotty sighed.

'What a comfort you are, Winnie.'

'I don't know about that, but you've certainly cheered me by giving me your company.'

Dotty stood up and began her usual disjointed quest for her belongings.

'Must you go so soon?'

'I really must. I feel so much better for the tea and sympathy. Where's my raincoat? And did I have a scarf?'

Winnie piloted her old friend into the hall, and helped her into her raincoat.

'Would you like me to walk back with you?'

'Not in this rain, Winnie dear. I promise you that I shall be quite all right now.'

'Then you must borrow the umbrella. No hurry for its return. It's an old one of Donald's that lives in the porch here for just such a downpour.'

Dotty accepted the umbrella, but before putting it up, she gave Winnie a rare kiss.

With something of her usual jauntiness she set off down the path. Beneath the great umbrella her thin legs in their wrinkled stockings splashed purposefully through the puddles.

Winnie watched until she vanished from sight across the darkening green, and then closed the front door and began to bolt and bar ready for the long night.

Twenty miles away, in the children's ward of the county hospital, the doctor on duty sat on Cyril Cooke's bed.

The boy was sitting up. His flushed face was between the doctor's two cold hands. They strayed over the cheeks, behind the tousled hair, and massaged the glands behind the ears and down the neck.

The child winced.

'Ever had mumps?' enquired the doctor.

Cyril, never a garrulous boy, was even less articulate in his present pain. He shook his head.

'Positive?'

He nodded, and emitted a squeak of agony.

The doctor stood up.

'Well, son, you've got 'em now,' he said laconically. 'See to him, nurse.'

PART THREE

The Outcome of Hostilities

15. *The Sad Affair of the Bedjacket*

The cold dry weather continued. Most nights there was frost, blackening the few remaining dahlias and stripping the last of the leaves from the trees.

'Do you think we might get a white Christmas?' asked Charles Henstock of Harold.

'No good asking me, my dear chap. Most of my Christmases were spent with the air conditioner going full blast, and the sweat still running down my back.'

'It does seem extraordinary,' ruminated the rector, 'how mild the winters are these days. I haven't been skating for years.'

'Skating?' Harold looked at his friend with new respect. 'Can you really skate?'

'Good heavens, yes! Most of us older folk can, you know. I learnt on Grantchester Meadows. A splendid chap from Durham taught me. He was up at Cambridge with me. I often wonder what became of him. He took part in an arctic expedition – that I do know – because he used to practise paddling his kayak on the Cam, mostly upside down. He loved it.'

'Paddling upside down, or skating?'

'Both really. He loved life – a great capacity for enjoyment. I think of him often, especially in cold weather.'

'And you think we might get some at Christmas?'

The rector sighed.

'I suppose not. It will be mild and muggy, I expect, and everyone will tell me the weather will make a full churchyard.'

He stopped. His chubby face began to pucker with concern.

'And that reminds me. I really came to tell you that there is a special meeting of the parochial church council at the rectory on the twenty-second. Can you manage it?'

'Of course,' said Harold.

'Seven-thirty, as usual.'

'I was afraid so,' replied Harold. 'I'll have an egg to my tea, as they say up north.'

'And a very sensible idea too,' responded Charles. 'I shall suggest it to Dimity. An empty stomach produces a lack of concentration, I find.'

'In me,' said Harold, 'it produces the most extraordinary noises.'

'You don't think,' said Charles, 'that this business is likely to go on for years? I really want to get things started. I read only the other day of a similar affair concerning a churchyard in East Anglia where controversy has continued for eighteen years.'

The rector turned troubled blue eyes upon his friend.

'*Eighteen years!*' he repeated. 'Can you bear to think of it, Harold? Why, I shall no doubt be among the blessed dead myself, if we take that time.'

'At least you wouldn't be worrying about it,' pointed out Harold reasonably.

On the last day of term, little Miss Fogerty carried her attaché case with extra care to school.

It contained two presents. One for Miss Watson, and a smaller one for the detestable Miss Potter.

Miss Fogerty had had mixed feelings about the presents, and was ashamed that she had harboured them. Never before had she felt anything but unalloyed pleasure at giving dear Miss Watson a Christmas present. This year, she had begun to wonder if she would give her one at all after the pain she had caused her during this most unpleasant term.

But the knitted bedjacket had been started last summer, long before Miss Potter arrived on the scene. The pattern was intricate, involving sixteen rows to each feather-and-shell design. Executed in pale pink three-ply wool it had taken Miss Fogerty many hours of fiddling work – and some of unpicking – to complete the garment, and even now she had her doubts about the scalloped edges to the collar and the width of the much-too-expensive satin ribbon which ensured modesty.

It should have been a labour of love. It started that way. It was in November, when the first sleeve was begun, that Miss Fogerty started to wonder if Miss Watson really deserved such efforts. She told herself that such thoughts were unworthy of a practising Christian, and continued to knit. But the thoughts intruded many times before the bedjacket was pressed and wrapped in Christmas paper.

However, she told herself as she hurried along to school, this was the season of goodwill, and Miss Watson would really appreciate her handiwork. It gave her a comfortable glow to think of her headmistress sitting up in bed reading, snugly embraced by the pink woolly.

As for Miss Potter, well – at Christmas one must be generous. A box of good linen handkerchiefs, bought at the church bazaar, accompanied the bedjacket, wrapped in similar Christmas paper but with a slightly smaller tag and a slightly more formal message. Privately, Miss Fogerty thought, the girl was very lucky.

Miss Fogerty put her attaché case on her desk and lifted out the two parcels. She carefully opened one end of Miss Watson's parcel to assure herself that the bow was uncrumpled. At that moment, Miss Potter entered.

'Brought your spencer?' she giggled, peering over Miss Fogerty's shoulder, in the rudest fashion.

Miss Fogerty closed the parcel swiftly.

'I fail to see anything funny about spencers,' she responded. 'But for your information I have not had occasion to wear mine as the weather has been so mild.'

Miss Potter had the grace to look slightly abashed. To tell the truth, she had been under the impression that such garments went out with Queen Victoria. That they were still winter wear at Thrush Green only confirmed her view that her present abode was abysmally behind the times.

Miss Fogerty produced the box of handkerchiefs and a creditable smile, and wished her young colleague a merry Christmas.

'Crumbs!' ejaculated that lady. 'Do we do all this present-giving? I haven't done anything about you or Miss Watson. But thank you very much,' she added hastily. 'I'll keep it till Christmas Day. We put all our presents round the tree, you know.'

The clanging of the hand bell announced that Miss Watson was in charge of the playground that day, and the two teachers hurried out to marshal their charges.

What with one thing and another, Miss Fogerty did not get the chance to give her headmistress the present until school was over. For one thing, Miss Watson was in the playground most of the time. Then the children were unusually boisterous, and there had been two infant puddles caused by pre-Christmas excitement (and *still* no sign of the emergency knickers, an unsolved mystery!), with the added complication of Albert Piggott's cat which had taken it into its head to explore the premises during the reading of 'The Tale of Mrs Tiggywinkle', thus distracting the children's already wayward attention.

Recognizing defeat, Miss Fogerty had allowed the children to give it half a bottle of school milk in the saucer lately occupied by mustard and cress, which the poor animal lapped so ravenously that, as she suspected, it was obvious that Piggott neglected it. Only when it had consumed half a digestive biscuit, the end of a ham sandwich, and a piece of chocolate pressed upon it by its doting hosts, did the animal settle to sleep by the tortoise stove and allow Miss Fogerty to resume her reading. Even then, she was exhorted to: 'Read soft, miss!' in case she disturbed the intruder.

The children had streamed home. Albert Piggott's cat, carefully wrapped in someone's scarf, was accompanied by a dozen well-wishers although, as Miss Fogerty had pointed out, the cat knew its own way home and would probably prefer to make the fifty-yard journey on foot.

Miss Potter put her head round the door and called: 'See you next term! Happy Christmas!' in a perfunctory manner, and promptly vanished, and Miss Fogerty and Miss Watson were, at last, alone in the building.

Miss Fogerty, back to her usual warm-hearted self in these familiar circumstances, put the parcel on Miss Watson's desk and stood back, smiling.

'Oh, Agnes dear, how *very* kind!' exclaimed the headmistress. 'And what pretty paper! You are always so clever about finding something that little bit different.'

Her eyes were sparkling. Miss Fogerty's hard thoughts had long ago vanished. The spirit of Christmas warmed her.

'Can I open it now, Agnes? I can never bear to wait until Christmas Day. I'm sure it's something wonderful.'

She began to undo the paper, Miss Fogerty watching indulgently. Just like a child, she thought, the same excitement, the same lovable impatience! Dear Miss Watson!

By now the parcel was opened and Miss Watson began to lift up the creation.

'Another bedjacket,' she cried with delight.

'*Another?*' quavered Miss Fogerty faintly.

'And what a beauty!' gabbled Miss Watson, struggling

valiantly to cover her slip. 'Did you do all this wonderful work yourself, Agnes dear?'

But Miss Fogerty was still stunned by the blow.

'You've had *another* bedjacket?' she queried, bemused. 'This Christmas? *Another* one?'

'Just a little thing from my brother,' said Miss Watson, torn painfully between Truthfulness and Kindness-to-Others, and attempting to sound airy at the same time. It was just such a situation, she thought desperately, that could bring on a stroke.

'It could never mean to me what this *perfect* present does, Agnes, I assure you! To think that you did every stitch – with your own hands!'

Not that she would have done every stitch with anybody else's hands, of course, thought poor distracted Miss Watson, but really, what could one say for comfort? Agnes looked positively shattered.

'How long did it take you?' she pressed, stroking the satin bow.

'I began it in June,' replied Miss Fogerty. She still sounded dazed.

'Come and have a cup of tea,' urged Miss Watson, 'before you go home. I'm afraid I haven't wrapped your present yet, Agnes dear. End of term, you know.'

'I must go,' said Miss Fogerty, as though in a trance, 'I too have a lot to do. I go away tomorrow.'

'Then I shall walk round this evening, if I may,' said Miss Watson. 'I shan't be leaving here until Christmas Eve. There is a Meeting Extraordinary of the Parochial Church Council on the twenty-second,' she continued importantly, 'so I shall stay to see that through.'

Little Miss Fogerty did not appear to hear her. She went blindly to her room, picked up her case and handbag, and walked out of the school door.

Behind her, sorely upset, Miss Watson set about wrapping the bedjacket with shaking hands.

Cold with shock, Miss Fogerty scuttled home through the dusk to her lodgings. She should never have said it! Never! Not even if she had received ten, twenty – nay, a *hundred* – bedjackets, she should never have uttered that dreadful, cruel, unforgivable word 'ANOTHER!'

To think of the hours, the weeks, the months of constant love – well, *almost* constant love, conceded Miss Fogerty honestly – which had gone into that bedjacket! And how had it been greeted? With admiration? With gratitude? Not a bit of it. It was 'Just Another Bedjacket'!

She could imagine the brother's 'little thing', of course. Some splendid quilted article, no doubt, of pure silk, possibly trimmed with swansdown, and costing as many guineas as she earned in a month's teaching. Oh, it was easy to give something splendid if one had a great deal of money, as she knew Miss Watson's brother had, but how much more worthwhile was her own hand-knitted beauty? Or so most people would think, Miss Fogerty told herself, putting her key in the lock. But not Miss Watson evidently! The pink bedjacket might be used for second-best, when the brother's superior article was at the cleaner's possibly, but that's what Miss Watson would think of it. Second best! *Another bedjacket!*

'Don't bother with a meal for me, Mrs White,' she called to her landlady. 'I'm catching the evening train after all.'

Equally unhappy, Miss Watson wandered about her school house suffering bitter remorse. Unable to face even her usual cup of tea, she watched the clock, determined to call at eight upon Agnes. By then she should have finished her meal and perhaps be feeling less upset.

Dear, oh dear, thought Miss Watson, struggling into her

coat, what a trial life was! She picked up the parcel which she had just wrapped. To the original present of Yardley's lavender water she had felt the need to add a box of Yardley's lavender bath cubes, providentially given to her by her cousin. There was something to be said for undoing one's Christmas presents as they arrived, she thought, as she smoothed the wrapping paper.

She walked through the darkness, across Thrush Green, still in a severe state of self-flagellation.

Why on earth had she said such a stupid thing? Why couldn't she simply have said: 'A bedjacket'? Why '*Another* bedjacket'? Why let slip that perfectly idiotic unnecessary, *wounding* word? Really, it made one wonder if the devil were still at large, popping such monstrous words into one's mouth! And how to explain? How to comfort poor Agnes? How to comfort herself? It was the sort of ghastly thing which would haunt her on sleepless nights; another to be added to those gaffes over the years which had power to torment her even though they had been committed over twenty years earlier.

Mrs White answered her knock.

'May I see Miss Fogerty, please?'

'Oh dear, you've just missed her,' cried the landlady. 'She left for the station half an hour ago.'

'But I thought –' began poor Miss Watson.

'So did I. But she said her friend would be pleased to see her tonight.'

'Have you got the friend's address?'

'I'm afraid not.'

Miss Watson shifted the parcel from one hand to the other in her agitation.

'Did she mention the name? Ida, or Elsie? She must have said something.'

Miss Watson's voice grew higher and higher. A lesser

woman might have sat on the doorstep and drummed her heels in wild hysteria. But Miss Watson was a headmistress and, although goaded almost beyond her limits, maintained some dignity.

'To tell you the truth,' said Mrs White, 'she seemed a bit upset. Not herself, as you might say.'

Miss Watson drew a deep breath.

'I can quite understand it,' she said. 'I will look forward to seeing her when she returns.'

'Would you want to leave the parcel?' enquired Mrs White. To her mind, Miss Watson looked a bit upset too. What could be the matter?

'Would you like to come in?' she asked. 'Sit down or anything?'

'No, thank you,' replied Miss Watson. 'I must go home. As for the parcel, I will give it to her myself later. There are one or two things to explain.'

She nodded politely, and set off in the darkness.

'She's aged a lot,' said Mrs White to her husband when she had closed the door.

'It's end of term,' replied Mr White sagely.

16. Getting Justice Done

The members of the parochial church council met in the dining-room at the rectory, and tried gallantly to look warm in that bleak apartment. The more prudent of them had added cardigans or waistcoats to their attire before setting out, and the aged churchwarden flatly refused to remove anything but his hat, with a courage which his fellow members secretly admired.

There were two vacant chairs, and the rector explained the matter at the outset.

'This meeting has been called, in the first place, because I have received the resignations of Mrs Cleary and Mr Hodge. I very much hope that they can be persuaded to change their minds, and we are here to discuss ways and means of meeting the views of the objectors.'

'I suppose it was to be expected,' said Miss Watson. She looked pale and dejected, thought Harold Shoosmith sitting opposite her. Glad to have a break from those children, he supposed. He'd sooner be in a trade than teaching, that was sure!

'It grieves me very much,' said the rector, 'to have this split among our good people.'

'You can't call eight a split,' broke in Harold.

'A disagreement then,' amended the rector. 'I wondered if you would think it a good idea if one of us met the objectors, or invited them to meet us, as a body, to see if we couldn't come to some amicable arrangement?'

'Sound 'em out, you mean?' said someone. 'Who are they anyway?'

The rector consulted the list while various voices recited names around the table.

'Besides Mr Hodge and his wife, and Mrs Cleary, there are Mr and Mrs Jones from "The Two Pheasants" and John and James Howard, and Martin Brewer.'

'You may not have noticed,' quavered the aged church-warden, 'that John and James Howard work for Mr Hodge, and live in one of his tied cottages.'

'Surely,' said Miss Watson, 'he wouldn't interfere in their religious convictions?'

'No, I'm not saying that. But they'd do as he told 'em.'

'And Martin Brewer,' pointed out someone else, 'works at Mrs Cleary's shop.'

'I thought he had a job as a van driver for the laundry,' said the rector, looking bewildered. 'I'm sure he calls here. A very pleasant young fellow, and understands all about decimal coins.'

'He doesn't drive now,' said Harold. 'He was disqualified for twelve months after an accident.'

'Deserved it too,' said the churchwarden. 'Doing seventy round the new estate. Dreadful!'

'Only according to the radar trap,' said another. 'I don't hold with those things. It isn't British, catching people when they're not looking.'

A heated debate might well have broken out, but the rector, familiar with the signs, banged the table and restored order.

'So Mrs Cleary gave him a job?'

'That's right. He's weighing up corn and grit and that, and loading the van for her.'

'I like oyster shell best,' said someone conversationally. 'My hens won't touch anything else, though my old dad used to sweep up the grit from the road, I remember, and our chickens at home seemed to thrive on it.'

'*And you think*,' said the rector, regaining control with some effort, 'that Martin might have signed because he felt grateful to her, or some such thing?'

'Could well be,' said Harold. 'Who does that leave?'

'Mr and Mrs Jones. I know he has been very forceful about it.'

'Only because of his Auntie May,' said the churchwarden. 'He thought the world of her. She's buried up near the yew tree. Nice bit of pink sandstone, she's got over her.'

'It occurs to me,' said Harold suddenly, 'that Mrs Cleary's family grave, and the Hodge graves are all close to the yew tree, and if the Jones's Auntie May is there too, we may be able to leave that small area undisturbed and still go ahead with levelling the rest.'

There was a respectful silence as the council digested this.

'What a happy thought!' said the rector.

'And Mrs Jones's Auntie May,' said the churchwarden, 'was a Hodge, of course. That's why she's there.'

'A Hodge?'

'Yes. May Hodge. Pretty girl, she was. Married Jones's uncle, and brought up Jones when his mother died. Now, she *was* a one! Proper harum-scarum! D'you remember that time she climbed up the rookery, George?'

He turned to a contemporary, wheezing with ancient laughter.

'*We are most grateful*,' cried the rector above the asthmatic noises, 'for bringing this to our attention. And how do you feel about Mr Shoosmith's suggestion that the area near the yew tree could be left?'

There were general murmurs of approval.

'That part,' said Miss Watson, suddenly coming to life, 'is so close to the new graveyard, which I think we agreed would remain as it is, that surely some beds with shrubs could make an attractive corner by the Hodge and Cleary graves, and at the same time provide a partial screen for the new graveyard.'

'It was supposed to be a privet hedge,' said the churchwarden. 'I well remember the row about green or golden, but the war came, you know, and we never got round to it.'

'I'm sure Miss Watson's idea could form the basis of an excellent scheme,' said Harold. 'But first things first. What about our eight objectors?'

'May I propose,' said Miss Watson, 'that some of us – or the rector himself, better still – approach them and see how they react?'

'Get 'em to withdraw their resignations,' growled George. 'Silly lot of nonsense! Old Percy Hodge is a useful chap and Mrs Cleary's all right when she's not on her high horse. I say, let the rector talk to 'em. The others will follow.'

'I should be only too happy to do what I can,' said Charles. 'This estrangement has been a great grief to me. And, of course, the sooner we get unity, then the sooner the faculty may be granted. If the objectors remain adamant, we must face considerable delays and considerable expense, as we are well aware. Nothing would please me more than to be able to resolve our differences here, at Thrush Green, without the unhappiness of going to court.'

'Then I propose that the rector sounds them out,' said Miss Watson.

'I'll second that,' said George.

'And what about some rough plan of the graves' area?' said Harold. 'Wouldn't it be a good thing to have something to show our objectors? They might be able to suggest further improvements.'

'Perhaps Miss Watson would help?' said Charles. 'It was her idea.'

'And Mr Shoosmith,' suggested another. 'He knows his onions when it comes to gardening.'

Thus it was left. Miss Watson and Harold would draft a rough plan for the rector to show the objectors, and it was left to him to see if some compromise could be arranged.

The meeting dispersed. Harold and Miss Watson walked together across the moonlit green.

'I go away tomorrow,' she told him, 'but I'll think about shrubs and so on which follow each other through the year, and perhaps we can meet when I get back in a few days' time.'

'I don't suppose Charles will have much time before that to do his visiting,' agreed Harold. 'Christmas keeps him pretty busy. No holiday for clergymen!'

They reached the school house gate.

'I hope you enjoy your break,' said Harold politely.

'Thank you,' replied Miss Watson. 'For once, I shall be glad to leave Thrush Green.'

As the rector had forecast, Christmas was mild and damp, and four of his parishioners told him to expect a spate of funerals within the next few weeks. It seemed to give them some satisfaction to impart the knowledge, which the good rector accepted with mingled resignation and fortitude.

Winnie Bailey spent the day with the Young family, in their handsome house so near her own. Ella and Dotty joined the Henstocks for tea, and the Hursts had gone to Frank's son in Wales for Christmas, leaving Tullivers and the cat in the care of Winnie Bailey.

In the week that followed, the inhabitants of Thrush Green turned, with some relief, to their usual way of life. Apart from dozens of Christmas cards blowing to the floor in every passing breeze and generally holding up the daily dusting, the main problem was to find a new way of presenting the remains of the turkey.

'I think curried turkey is the best way of finishing it up,' said Dimity one morning, when she was taking coffee at her former abode with Ella and Winnie.

'Not bad,' agreed Ella, 'but I prefer it with mushrooms

and white sauce. Easy to do too. Or shepherd's pie, of course.'

'The fact is,' said Dimity, 'that *any* turkey dish, after five days of it, tends to pall. I'm *longing* for a steak and kidney pie!'

'I didn't buy a turkey this year,' said Winnie.

'Then you're extremely lucky,' her friends told her.

'And now we've January to look forward to,' sighed Ella. 'Talk about the January blues! What with the bills, and the general damp and gloom, and so long to wait for spring – it does get one down!'

'I cheer myself up,' said Dimity, 'by tidying a cupboard. It makes me feel so virtuous and efficient.'

'I buy a new pair of shoes,' said Winnie.

'A packet of bourbon biscuits peps me up,' said Ella. 'Or putting out a new tablet of soap. Very therapeutic, putting out a new tablet of soap, I find.'

'As good as a day in the garden?' asked Winnie.

'Far better, in January,' replied Ella emphatically. 'Have some more coffee? I asked Dotty to come up, but she doesn't seem to want to be sociable these days. Worrying about that confounded court appearance, I suppose. One thing, the Cooke boy is home again, I hear, and getting over the mumps. That must ease poor old Dotty's conscience.'

Winnie said nothing. Dotty's confidences would never be disclosed, but she knew that she would never forget the depths of misery in which she had found her old friend on that dark afternoon.

'Well, a court case *is* worrying,' said Dimity. 'I think we're all worried for her. It will be a good thing when it comes up in a fortnight or so, and we can all forget the wretched business.'

There was one person who was more worried than most about Dotty's case, and that was the clerk to the Lulling magistrates. A comparative newcomer to the area – he had moved from a busy London court a mere ten years earlier – he could not be expected to know the ramifications of relatives, employers and employed, and other complications of rural communities.

To give him his due, he readily discovered the difficulties within a few months of taking up his appointment. He tackled his job with outstanding ability and good humour, and was readily accepted by a community which normally took some time to acknowledge a newcomer as 'one of us'.

He was used to the occasional 'sitting back' of a magistrate in cases where the defendant was known to, related to or employed by that particular justice. The case of Dotty Harmer was creating even more trouble.

Six of the twelve Lulling magistrates stated roundly that they could not possibly sit in judgement upon Dotty. Not only had all six been instructed – painfully, sometimes – by Dotty's notable father at the local grammar school, which would not have mattered greatly, but all knew Dotty from childhood days.

'Used to play tennis with her, didn't we, Bob?' said one farmer to his fellow magistrate. 'She never did get round to serving over-arm, but she was deadly at the net.'

The fishmonger cried off because Miss Harmer was one of his best customers 'owning all those cats'.

Another justice was her builder. Another had been employed by her family for a time. Another claimed that he was 'a sort of cousin' and poor Mr Pearson, the clerk, could see it was going to be hell's delight to find three justices willing to hear the case.

Urgent telephone calls to the remaining six justices brought little help. One was waiting to go into hospital, and a third, the youngest newly-appointed matron, confessed that she had just discovered that she was to have a baby. At that moment, Mr Pearson's coffee arrived, and he suspended operations to fortify himself.

Really, he thought, stirring pensively, it was all very fine for Lord Chancellors to urge the appointment of young females to the bench, but it did complicate things! He stopped stirring as a thought struck him. If she had only just discovered her condition, then it was reasonable to suppose that her confinement was some months distant. Consequently, there seemed to be no reason why she should not attend court on the day of Dotty's case. He resolved to try the last three justices, and to ring back to Mrs Fothergill if he could not gather three together.

He finished his coffee and tried again. This time he was lucky. Mr Jardine could come. His wife, he believed, knew Miss Harmer at the Field Club, but he had only met her once. No, he had no objection to sitting. Dam' it all, if one were to sit back every time someone slightly known appeared before one, it would be impossible to conduct a court at all!

Mr Pearson agreed heartily, thanked Mr Jardine sincerely, and set about the ensnaring of Lady Winter.

That lady said she had a great many engagements on at the time of Dotty's case. When was it? One moment, she would consult her diary. It was not very convenient as she was organizing a Charity Ball that evening and would be getting her hair done. Would Mr Pearson care to come? The tickets were five pounds each and she was personally making the punch.

Mr Pearson, with his usual diplomacy, turned down the invitation, and then threw himself into urgent pleading, explaining the terrible predicament he was in. Lady Winter, who had a soft spot for the clerk, allowed herself to be persuaded, and agreed to make her hair appointment in the late afternoon instead of the morning. No, she had not the pleasure of knowing Miss Harmer, although she had heard of her father. Who hadn't?

'One to go!' murmured Mr Pearson, twirling the dial with a pencil.

Mrs Lucy answered the call. She was sorry but Edgar was out, should he ring when he came in?

Mr Pearson gave her the date of the hearing and said he would try Mrs Fothergill, and let the Lucys know the outcome.

'I must tell you,' said Mrs Lucy, 'we are in the most awful muddle at the moment. Edgar's father has been taken ill, and we are setting off to see him later today.'

His father was in Huddersfield, added Mrs Lucy, but, from what the doctor said, would be leaving for Higher Things before long. Edgar, as the only son, would have everything to clear up.

Mr Pearson condoled, promised to ring again, and returned to Mrs Fothergill. The clock told him that he had spent an hour in his searchings, and a pile of papers awaited his attention.

Mrs Fothergill said she could come *easily*. Mr Pearson sighed with relief.

'And you don't know Miss Harmer?'

'I once helped to push her car into a side street, but I was one of about six others. She doesn't know me, and I've never met her otherwise.'

'Good,' said the clerk. 'That's three of you rounded up.'

'I've heard of her father, of course,' said Mrs Fothergill.

'Who hasn't?' agreed Mr Pearson. After mutual felicitations, they rang off.

'Just the Lucys once more,' said Mr Pearson, strong again.

Humming blithely, he dialled for the last time.

*

On the same morning as the clerk to the justices was engaged in telephoning, Charles Henstock set out from the rectory to pay his appointed call on Percy Hodge.

He approached his task with some trepidation. Rumour had it that Percy Hodge, when crossed, could be a formidable adversary. Charles did not doubt it. The removal of himself and his family from church, the wording of his resignation and the obstinate set of Percy's mouth all told of a stubborn character. He might prove impossible to move.

But the rector, despite his misgivings, went steadfastly upon his way. If Percy could be persuaded to fall in with these new suggestions, then he felt sure that the other objectors would follow suit.

He had debated with himself about the advisability of calling upon Percy first. Dimity had suggested that it would be politer to visit Mrs Cleary, on the 'ladies-first' principle.

Charles had wondered about the Joneses'. He had a feeling that, despite his blusterings, Jones might give way more readily, especially when he had seen the suggested plans, so neatly executed by Harold.

But, after much cogitation, the rector had decided to crack the toughest nut first. For one thing, Percy would resent being put after anyone else. If the others had agreed, it would make him doubly adamant about resisting. The rector, innocent in so many things, was wise in discerning the motives which stirred human passions.

He came to the farmhouse gate and, like all good countrymen, went to the back door of the house to knock for admission.

Percy himself answered the door.

'Come in,' he said. 'I've been expecting you!'

With pleasure or anger, wondered the rector? He stepped bravely into the lion's den.

17. The Rector in Action

'Sorry I'm a bit late,' cried Betty Bell. 'Been trying to get that new floor to rights next door, and forgot the time.'

'Don't worry,' said Harold. 'I didn't realize you had to call in at the school during the holidays.'

'Lord love you,' responded Betty, 'that's my busiest time! I mean, term-time it gets a lick and a promise, as you might say, except for Friday nights. But I gives the whole place a thorough scrub through during the holidays.'

'I should have known.'

'I don't see why you should. Selling things was your line. Floors is mine. But you never saw such a pig's breakfast as that new floor. That young teacher lets 'em do as they like, from what I can see. There's glue and paint and plasticine and ground-up crayon, and enough bubble-gum to keep you going for a month.'

'Not me,' said Harold, shuddering.

'Well, you know what I mean. Now, Miss Fogerty's room is a real treat to do. Everything left tidy, chairs on desks ready for me to sweep, nice bit of paper lining the waste paper basket so there's no pencil shavings and that dropping through. She's even got a little brush to sweep up the coke bits! Takes me half the time to do her room.'

'Bully for Miss Fogerty!' said Harold, making for the refuge of his study. It was plain that Betty was in full spate today.

'Well, that's as it should be. Children wants training. I know my mum never let us leave things about. If we did, they was thrown in the pit, up the end of our garden. We never had no dustbins in those days. I can remember rescuing an old dolly of mine, in the pouring rain. She never looked the same after a night in the pit, but it learnt me a lesson, all the same.'

'I had a nurse,' replied Harold, halted in his tracks, 'who threw my things on the back of the fire. I can remember watching a lead soldier – a cavalry officer, too – melting away. It broke my heart.'

'That was downright cruel!' cried Betty indignantly. 'I hope she got the sack!'

'She did, as soon as my father realized she was sampling his brandy,' said Harold, and made his escape.

At much the same time, across the green, Jenny arrived at Winnie Bailey's. Jenny very rarely spoke unless she had something worthwhile to say, but this morning she looked unusually animated.

'Had good news, Jenny?' asked her mistress.

'Yes. Willie Bond brought a letter for the old folks. They've got a new house at last. One of those old people's homes the council built.'

Jenny's honest plain face glowed with pleasure.

'How wonderful! Just what they've always wanted. And when can they move in?'

'About a month's time. There's got to be an inspection or something, to make sure everything works. As soon as that's done they can go in.'

'And what about your present house, Jenny?'

'Well, that'll come down. All our row will, and a good thing too. It's been condemned for years now. We knew it would happen one day.'

'So what will you do?'

'I'll face that when the time comes,' said Jenny cheerfully. 'I'll find a room somewhere I expect. Might even go nursing – I did a bit once – and I could live in the hostel.'

'Would you want to do that?'

'Not really,' said Jenny. 'Besides, I'm a bit old. I don't know if they'd have me. But I shall find something all right. Just get the old folks settled, and I'll start thinking.'

She went humming upstairs to clean the bathroom, while Winnie turned over in her mind a plan which had been lurking there for some time.

It continued to engage her thoughts as she sat knitting that afternoon. Her dislike of being alone after dark had certainly diminished as the weeks went by, but she could not honestly say that she was completely carefree. She had wondered if it would be sensible to let two rooms upstairs. She would still have a spare bedroom, quite enough for the modest entertaining she proposed to do in her widowed state.

The two rooms adjoined. Both had wash-basins, one of which could be changed to a kitchen sink. There would be plenty of room for an electric stove and for cupboards, and it would convert easily into a comfortable kitchen.

The room next door was larger and would make an attractive bed-sitting room. Both rooms overlooked the green and were light and sunny.

The difficulty was, who would be acceptable? Winnie did not want a married couple, and such a minute flat would not be suitable for people with babies or pets. A single man might be useful for attacking the marauders that Winnie feared, but then he might expect his washing and ironing to be done, and his socks darned, and Winnie was beginning to feel rather too old for such mothering.

No, a pleasant single woman was the answer! One with a job during the day, who enjoyed looking after her small domain, and who did not demand too much attention from her landlady. The financial side was something of a problem to Winnie, who had not the faintest idea what should be charged. Nor did she know if there should be some legal document setting out the terms upon which landladies and lodgers agreed.

And then, supposing they did not get on? It was common knowledge that one really had to live with people before one knew them properly. Look at that terrible Brides-in-the-Bath man! No, thought Winnie, don't look at him, with dusk already beginning to fall!

She rose to draw the curtains and to switch on the lamp. Across the green, she saw the rector marching purposefully toward 'The Two Pheasants'. Unusual, thought Winnie. Perhaps he was calling on his sexton, Albert Piggott, or on Harold Shoosmith nearby.

But the rector was opening the wicket gate at the side of the public house, and vanished from sight.

Winnie resumed her seat and her knitting. Over the past few weeks she had come to the conclusion that the person she would most like to share her home was quiet, devoted Jenny. That is, of course, if she would come.

And now, with this morning's news, it looked as though there were a chance. She would await her opportunity, and put the proposition before Jenny. How lovely, thought Winnie, letting her knitting fall and looking at the leaping flames, if she agreed! The bogey of loneliness would be banished, and the tiresome business of trying to find out what would be a fair rent would also be solved, for Jenny would live there rent-free.

Winnie allowed herself to indulge in happy daydreams for some five minutes, and then pulled herself together sharply. It was no good getting too hopeful. Jenny might well have other plans, besides the vague ones she had mentioned, and, in any case, a shared home at Thrush Green might be abhorrent to her.

Well, time would show. Winnie picked up her knitting

again, determined to remain cool-headed over the whole affair. But hope warmed her throughout the evening.

Charles Henstock, whom Winnie had glimpsed from her window, was making the second of his visits that day on the vexed question of the graveyard.

Percy Hodge had greeted him somewhat grimly, but had ushered him into the parlour, in deference, presumably, to his cloth.

Frankly, Charles would have preferred the kitchen, where the life of the farmhouse revolved. For one thing, it was warm and cheerful, a great room dominated by an immense scrubbed table, and an Aga cooker which dispensed heat and a delicious smell of baking bread.

The parlour was neither warm nor cheerful. Percy switched on the electric fire as he entered, but the rector might just as well have been in his own study for all the comfort it gave.

Two enormous pictures of stags standing in water, against a background of Highland mountains, dominated the walls, and a vast three-piece suite, upholstered in drab moquette, filled most of the floor space. The linoleum, meant to represent, not very convincingly, a traditional Turkish carpet in crimson and blue, gleamed icily.

'Take a seat,' said Percy. 'I take it you've come about me not coming to church.'

Percy was nothing if not direct, thought Charles.

'Not quite that, although we've all missed you and the family at our services. You are still opposed, no doubt, to the churchyard scheme?'

'Of course I am,' said Percy forcefully. 'It beats me why more people didn't sign. You hear enough about it in the village, but people are afraid to put their names down.'

'Are you sure? I shouldn't like to think that was so.'

'Well, maybe they talk that way when I'm there. I don't know. Folk will try to run with the hare and the hounds, and to my mind you can't do both. You know my feelings on the subject. I'm against the thing.'

'Tell me your strongest objection.'

'My strongest objection is having the resting place of my forefathers disturbed.'

'And if it were to remain undisturbed, would you then approve the project?'

'How d'you mean?'

Percy looked suspicious. Charles spread his hands towards the meagre heat from the electric stove, and began to outline the suggested proposals. He explained things gently and patiently, his brow furrowed with concern, and towards the end of the explanation, he took the sketch map from his pocket.

Percy's expression grew grimmer as he listened.

'Trying to buy me off, are you?' he said at last.

For the first time in Percy's life, he saw a flash of anger cross the rector's face.

'I should never have imagined that you would stoop to such a remark,' he said. 'It does you no credit, and is insulting to me. There is conflict in my parish which I am trying to stop. No one can ever know the grief which it is causing me.'

He rose as if to go.

'Sit down, sir, sit down,' urged Percy, looking uncomfortable. 'I shouldn't have said that. I'm sorry. I know you well enough to know you're dead straight. Sit down, and tell me more.'

The rector resumed his seat.

'When I was a schoolboy,' he said, more calmly, 'we had a prayer about being careful not to mistake bluntness for frankness, and obstinacy, I think it was, for constancy. You know, Percy, I have always respected your principles, but you must face the fact that we all have to make compromises in this life, if we are to live amicably together. All I am doing is to show you how willing we are to settle things for the best. Even hares and hounds have to shake down in the same world.'

'Let's have a look at the plan,' said Percy, holding out his hand for Harold's rough sketch. He studied it in silence, while the rector observed him. A whirring noise from the wall clock behind him caused him to turn. A wooden cuckoo burst from its lair and shouted three times. In the distance the cows lowed. It would soon be milking time.

'What happens,' said Percy, returning the sketch, 'if we don't change our minds?'

The rector told him of delays, expense, the possibility of a consistory court, and the usual procedure in such a case.

Percy listened attentively.

'Well, I'm not going to say now one way or the other, but I'll think things over, and let you know. I'm not an unreasonable man, I hope, but I want to do what's right.'

'I'm sure of that.'

'And I'll tell my two men what you've told me,' went on Percy. 'They'll do as I do, of course.'

Charles felt a tremor of dismay.

'I shouldn't want them to go against their consciences. You know that, I feel sure. They must weigh things up, just as you are going to do.'

'I'll see to them,' said Percy, and with this somewhat ambiguous remark, he saw the rector to the door.

It was not much, thought Charles Henstock, as he walked home to Thrush Green, but at least he had not had the door slammed in his face. He bitterly regretted his own flash of anger, but Percy's remark had cut him cruelly. Perhaps, however, his own outburst had cleared the air. Certainly, Percy seemed more reasonable after it.

He went into the long corridor leading to the kitchen, expecting to find Dimity, but remembered that she had proposed to go shopping in Lulling. The kettle purred on the stove, and he wondered whether to make tea.

It was now half-past three. This would be a good time to call on the Joneses'. Lunch would be over, and the pub would be closed until six.

Heartened by the glimmer of hope given him by Percy, he decided to try his luck, and set off.

Mr Jones was alone and showed the rector into a sitting-room which was the very opposite of Percy Hodge's.

'The wife's gone shopping,' explained Mr Jones. 'We don't get much time for that sort of thing. Very tied with a pub, you know, but it suits me.'

He indicated an armchair and Charles sank down into depths so soft that he wondered if he would ever be able to rise again. There were flowers everywhere. The covers were ablaze with roses, the walls with wistaria hanging on trellis. On the mantelpiece, above the roaring fire, was an arrangement of plastic flowers and fern, where tulips, delphiniums, crocuses and chrysanthemums rioted together in defiance of the seasons.

Even the kettle-holder, hanging on a hook by the fireside, had a posy of forget-me-nots on it, and the spaniel which lay at their feet, Charles remembered, was called Blossom.

He began to feel guilty, a worm in the bud, a serpent in this bower of flowers.

'What can I get you, padre?' asked his host. 'Whisky? Drop of rum to keep out the cold?'

'No, nothing, thank you. I shall be having some tea very soon. How snug you are in here!'

'We need somewhere comfortable when we're on our

own,' said the landlord. 'Our job means you've got to be among a crowd most of the time. And standing too. It's good to sink down in here when we can.'

'I've just come from Percy Hodge's,' said the rector, coming straight to the point.

Mr Jones began to look wary.

'About the churchyard? What's Perce say?'

The rector told him the gist of their conversation, and handed over the sketch map.

'Could look rather nice,' said the landlord slowly. Charles's spirits rose. He remembered that Mr Jones was a great gardener.

'If it did come about,' he said cautiously, 'we should need some advice about planting and so on. At the moment, Miss Watson and Mr Shoosmith are thinking about shrubs.'

Perhaps Charles had gone too far and too fast. The landlord's face tightened, and he handed back the piece of paper.

'What happens if we still object?' he said. Charles was reminded that Percy and this man were related.

He told him. Mr Jones nodded.

'You don't want to get mixed up with lawyers,' he said, at last. 'You'll have Thrush Green in debt for years if you take this matter to some court or other. I'm not saying yes or no, but I can see your point, and I reckon we ought to settle this business here in the village ourselves.'

'Exactly my feelings,' said the rector.

'What did Perce say?' he repeated.

'He said much the same as you are saying, that he wanted time to think about it.'

'And what, padre, do *you* think? As man to man, I mean?'

'I want the churchyard to look beautiful, a fitting place for the loved dead here. But I want harmony among the living. If we give and take – all of us – I think we can resolve our difficulties. That's why I'm approaching all the objectors.'

'Well, you've got some pluck, that I will say, and I promise to think it over. Mind you, I've shot my mouth off about it pretty strong in the bar here, but I'm not above changing my mind if it's the right thing to do.'

'It isn't a sign of weakness,' said the rector, attempting to struggle from the chair, 'rather the contrary.'

'Here,' said Mr Jones, proffering a hand, 'let's give you a haul up.'

The two men stood on the hearthrug smiling at each other. A smell of singeing made the rector move suddenly from such unaccustomed heat.

'Well, I'll be off, and leave you to your rest,' said Charles. He turned at the door.

'You'll let me know your decision, won't you?' he pleaded. 'I care very much about the outcome.'

'You shall know before the week's out,' promised the landlord.

At Tullivers, that evening, Frank Hurst broached again the thorny subject of Jeremy's schooling. Little had been said about it since their earlier difference of opinion, but Phyllida remained determined to keep the boy at home for a few more years, and Frank was equally desirous of the child going to his own old prep school, which he remembered happily.

'Tom's taking his youngest down to Ribbleworth next week,' he announced, when Phil returned from putting Jeremy to bed. 'He's sitting the entrance exam.'

'Is he?' said Phil guardedly.

'Do just come and have a look at the place,' persuaded Frank. 'I know how you feel at the moment, but indulge me, and pay a visit with me. You may change your mind. I could ring the head, and make an appointment.'

Phil hesitated. It seemed a complete waste of time to her. She was against the principle of wresting young boys from their homes, particularly in Jeremy's case where the child had had some tough knocks in his short life and was getting over them well in his present happy circumstances.

On the other hand, she could see Frank's point, and it would be unkind to ignore his wishes.

'Very well,' she agreed. 'But it will have to be a positive paradise to convince me. You know that well enough.'

Frank laughed.

'I'll take the risk. Here, sit down, and I'll bring you a glass of sherry.'

18. A Cold Spell

Little Miss Fogerty returned from her Christmas holiday two days before term began.

She had not intended staying so long with her friend Isobel, but had been persuaded to extend her visit. Isobel, recently widowed, said that she would be grateful for her company, and Miss Fogerty, touched and flattered that she should be needed, readily agreed to stay.

'Besides,' added Isobel, 'you don't look as fit as you usually do. I expect you have been over-working.'

'It has been a trying term,' admitted Miss Fogerty, but wild horses would not have dragged from her the true miseries which had caused the shadows under her eyes, and the wretchedly disturbed nights.

She certainly began to feel better after a week or so with dear Isobel. The house was large and warm. The spare room had a bed which was plump and soft, and a bathroom of its own, which Miss Fogerty considered the height of luxury. The bath sheet alone gave Miss Fogerty an exquisite sense of being cosseted. It was pale blue, and so large and fluffy that it could wrap her small frame twice round, and then have a generous wrap-over. Mrs White's bath towels were less than half the size, and made of some harsher striped towelling which simply pushed the water from one part of one's body to another without doing its proper job of absorption.

It was delightful too to be taken everywhere by car. Not that Miss Fogerty was lazy, nor that she underestimated the well-being which results from healthy exercise, but in the depths of winter the taking of a brisk walk so often meant cold fingers and toes. It was true too, as Isobel said, that she was not feeling as well as she normally did, and to lean back in a comfortable car seat and watch the wintry world roll by, without any effort, was exceedingly pleasant.

When the time came to depart she felt all the better for her rest, and tried to tell her friend how much the break had meant to her.

'I've loved having you,' Isobel said, gazing up at the carriage window which framed Miss Fogerty's small face topped by a neat beige felt hat. 'Now, do as I say, and take a tonic while the winter lasts.'

The train began to move.

'And wrap up warmly,' cried Isobel more loudly. 'We're going to get a cold snap.'

The two friends waved until a curve in the line separated them. Miss Fogerty pulled up the window, and sank back into her seat. She took out a handkerchief and blew her nose. Emotion was one cause of this operation, but a piercing east wind was a greater one.

Two hours later, as she trudged from the station through Lulling High Street, she shivered in the icy blast which swept that thoroughfare. It seemed colder still at Thrush Green at the top of the hill.

She looked across at the school house. A light shone from the sitting-room window. No doubt Miss Watson was reading, or perhaps enjoying her tea by the fire. On other occasions, Miss Fogerty might have been tempted to tap on the door, but not now.

She put down her case and rammed on the sensible felt hat more firmly. Only another few yards and she would be home again!

She picked up her case and set off once more. With any luck, Mrs White would have a tea tray ready for her in her room. She could have the kettle boiling on the ring in less than five minutes.

With a pang, Miss Fogerty recalled the log fire, the plump

cushions, and the silver tea pot which had graced the tea time hour at Isobel's.

Ah well! It would not do to become too fond of soft living, she told herself firmly, and after all, this was her home and all her dear familiar things would be there to welcome her.

The first fat white snowflake, drifting as easily as a wind-blown feather, fluttered to the ground as she opened the gate. By the time the kettle boiled, the sky was awhirl with flakes, spinning past the window, veiling the garden, tumbling dizzily, helter-skelter, as though some gigantic feather bed had burst in the dark leaden sky above.

Isobel was right, thought Miss Fogerty, sipping her tea gratefully. Wintry weather indeed, and from the look of things, more to come!

Thrush Green awoke to a white world. The Cotswold stone walls were covered in snow four or five inches deep. The gateposts wore white tam-o'-shanters, and Nathaniel Patten held out his snow-covered book and gazed upon his birth-place from under a crown of snow.

The green itself was a vast unsullied expanse. The wind had blown a great drift against the railings of St Andrew's church, so that only the spikes were visible. Their black zig-zag, and the dark trunks of the chestnut avenue, served to accentuate the dazzling whiteness of the scene.

It was still snowing when the rector arose and went downstairs to make tea. His breath billowed before him in the chill of the house, and he was glad to gain the comparative warmth of the kitchen.

The cat stretched, mewed, and leapt upon the table asking to be let out of the window. The rector gazed up at the whirling flakes. They fluttered against his face like icy moths. One fell into his open mouth, and he remembered suddenly how he used to rush about in the snow, as a child, catching the snow flakes on his tongue, and then how he had seized a handful from a wall and had crammed it into his mouth, spluttering excitedly, and crying: 'You can *eat* it! You can *eat* it!'

How beautiful it was! He closed the window, and watched two sparrows alight on the roof of Dimity's bird tray. Their tiny claws formed hieroglyphics in the snow, like foreign letters printed on the virgin page.

Beautiful indeed, thought the rector, fetching the teapot, but how cold! Perhaps he needed a thicker dressing-gown. His present one had been given to him long ago by his dear first wife. No doubt twenty years of wear had worn it rather threadbare. He looked at the garment with unusual attention. The cuffs were certainly quite frayed, and he seemed to remember that the whole surface had once been fluffy. Now it was smooth, and almost worn through at the elbows. Well, it would probably last another few years, thought Charles cheerfully, advancing upon the boiling kettle.

He was about to pick up the tray when the cat returned to the window sill demanding entry. Its coat was flecked with snowflakes, its eyes wild at finding itself in this unaccustomed element.

It shot in, and ran to the stove, shaking itself spasmodically, and uttering little cries of dismay. Outside, the snow hissed sibilantly against the window pane, and a great cushion of it fell with a flurry from an overloaded branch nearby.

Hitching up his dilapidated dressing-gown, the rector lifted his tray and made for the stairs.

The snow was still thick on the ground when term began. Miss Fogerty wore her wellington boots and some extra thick ribbed woollen stockings. She also wore her spencer underneath her sensible brown twin-set, for she knew, only too well, how draughty Thrush Green School could be when the wind was in the north east.

She had hoped that Miss Watson might call, but no doubt she was busy with preparations for the term, she thought charitably. In any case, the weather had not been very tempting, and most people had been glad to stay by the fireside.

Although the memory of the bedjacket still had power to cause Miss Fogerty some unhappiness, the balm of Isobel's hospitality had taken some of the sting from the wound. It was no good dwelling on the affair, she told herself, as she trotted through the snow to school that first morning. We have to work together. We are two grown women, and we must treat the incident as closed.

Nevertheless, she could not quite overcome her uneasiness at meeting Miss Watson again. Their last meeting, after all, had been so dreadfully painful. She listened for her head-mistress's footsteps as she hung up her coat and removed her wet wellingtons. Her little black house-shoes hung in their cretonne bag, inside the map cupboard, where she had placed them on that last disastrous day.

She was buttoning the straps when Miss Watson entered. The headmistress held out a parcel wrapped in Christmas paper.

'Much too late, Agnes dear, I'm afraid,' she said, smiling. 'I did call to give it to you, but I just missed you, so Mrs White told me. Had a good holiday?'

Miss Fogerty was relieved to see the smile, and to realize that they were back – or nearly so – to their normal friendly relationship. It was a mercy not to have an emotional scene, and yet Miss Fogerty could not help thinking that it might have been even better if Miss Watson had shown some remorse for that unfeeling remark which had caused her assistant such misery. It would have been nice if Miss Watson had begged for forgiveness, and had recognized her own culpability. Not that she wanted her headmistress to *grovel*, but after all, it would have been truly heroic if she could have brought herself to apologize or to explain.

However, thought Miss Fogerty, undoing the parcel with little cries of gratitude, perhaps 'Least said, soonest mended' was Miss Watson's motto, and a very sensible one too.

'My favourite perfume!' cried Miss Fogerty. 'You couldn't have given me anything more welcome.'

'Well, it isn't anywhere near as splendid a present as yours to me, Agnes, but I'm glad you like it.'

The bell clanged outside.

'Miss Potter's on time for once,' commented Miss Watson, and the two teachers hurried to greet their pupils in the lobby.

Nothing more was said about the bedjacket, and Miss Fogerty resolutely put aside any little feelings of rancour as being quite unworthy of a sensible middle-aged school-teacher.

It was during this wintry spell that Frank and Phil Hurst went to visit the prep school at which Frank had been so happy.

Phil resolved to enjoy the outing and to try and bring an open mind to the question of Jeremy's boarding. The sun came through now and again, lighting the snow into un-believable beauty and casting blue shadows under the trees.

They lunched on the way and drove up the long road to the school about two o'clock. A group of little boys in very large boots rushed about frenziedly between two sets of rugby posts, urged on by a hefty young man girt about with striped scarves.

The boys, to Phil's pitying gaze, looked blue with cold and

grossly underclad and underfed. But she was prudent enough to make no comment as they drove to the front door.

A homely touch, which cheered her, was the sight of a splendid snowman on the lawn, also wearing a striped scarf, a dilapidated mortar-board, and a clay pipe. Some wag had thrust a stick, where his arm might be, to represent a cane.

A pasty-faced maid, very short of breath, answered the door, and led the way, puffing, through a maze of corridors to the head's study at the back of the building.

'Used to lead off the front hall,' observed Frank to his wife. 'Can't think why they take us all round this way.'

'The old study's a staff room now,' volunteered the maid wheezily.

She stopped at a door and knocked.

'Come in,' came a shout.

'Mr and Mrs Never-Caught-Your-Name,' announced the maid.

The head welcomed them boisterously.

'Frank Hurst,' said Frank, 'and my wife. I'm an old boy. We rang some time ago, you remember.'

'Indeed, yes. Indeed, yes. So delighted you could come. My wife, unfortunately, has had to go to a meeting. Now, let me see . . .'

He began to shuffle papers on a very untidy desk. Phil sat back and looked around her. The passages which they had traversed had been somewhat grubby, she had noticed. This study was not much cleaner, and the head himself, though handsome once, no doubt, now looked in need of tidying up, she thought.

His tie was greasy, his coat spotted, and his suede shoes needed brushing. Not a very good example to the boys! The only feature which brightened his appearance was a gold tooth, which dominated the conversation to such an extent, that Phil found herself making a strong effort to direct her gaze well above it into the head's eyes.

After a few reminiscences Frank turned to the subject of Jeremy, entrance examinations, further schooling and present attainments.

'And now you must come and see how we live and work,' said the head. 'Mothers always like to see the kitchens and dormitories.'

They followed him back through the labyrinth of corridors until they came to a fine oak staircase. It was badly splintered on the treads, and the banister felt sticky. Phil thought how sad it was to see such a splendid stairway so unloved. Once, it must have been a family's pride, suitably furnished with a fine carpet, and cared for with brush and dustpan and polish by a generation or so of devoted housemaids.

They were shown into several dormitories. Bare boarded, apart from a single strip of thin carpet between the two rows of beds, and curtainless, they appeared to Phil unbelievably bleak. Red blankets did little to mitigate the cheerlessness and the sight of battered teddy bears and other much-loved toys on the beds only added to the poignancy of the scene.

'And this is matron's abode,' said the head leading the way through an elementary surgery-cum-bathroom to an inner sitting-room. Here an auburn-haired young woman hastily rose, and stubbed out a cigarette before greeting them.

'Marjorie,' said the head, 'Mr and Mrs Hurst. Their boy David may be coming here.'

'Jeremy,' said Phil automatically.

The head laughed heartily, the gold tooth glinting.

'Jeremy! Jeremy, of course.'

'He'll love it here,' volunteered matron. 'They are all ever so happy, aren't they, Peter?'

'I think we can say so,' agreed the head, 'I think we can say so.'

Did he say everything twice, wondered Phil? What a perfect person for rude little boys to mimic!

'Might have a day or two feeling a bit homesick at first,' admitted matron, stroking her well-filled mauve jumper while the head eyed her approvingly, 'but we soon jolly them out of that.'

'That's true. That's very true,' agreed the head.

They were led on their tour. The classrooms were large and shabby. The desks were well-carved, the easels splintered, the blackboards needed resurfacing and over all hung the indefinable smell of boy – a fatty, sweaty, chalky smell.

They went out into the snowy wastes to look at the workshop, the gym, the swimming pool and the new half-built pavilion. The little boys had finished their games session and now ran past them, tumbling about together like puppies, sniffing with the cold, hitting each other playfully.

'Sir!' they shouted, when they saw the head, as they passed. Their breath blew around their heads in silver clouds. One or two smiled at Phil, some so young that their front milk teeth had gone. Their gappy smiles made her think of Jeremy, with a sharp pang.

They returned to the car.

'You'll have some tea?' invited the head, but Phil said that they had such a long journey that she felt they had better not stay longer.

'The playroom?' said Frank suddenly. 'What's happened to the playroom?'

'We use it as a science lab. now,' said the head. 'Needed the space, you know.'

They made their farewells, the head's gold tooth flashing in the winter sunlight, and drove homeward.

'Gone to seed a bit,' said Frank thoughtfully.

Phil did not reply. She had found the whole visit thoroughly depressing. It only strengthened her conviction that Jeremy would be better off at home.

They drove in silence for a mile or two.

'Of course, we saw it at its worst,' continued Frank. 'Always looks grim – a school in winter.'

They drove through a small town. The snow had been swept into two grubby mountain ranges, one each side of the main street.

'Didn't take to the head particularly,' went on Frank. 'But there, no one would come up to our old man! Rough luck having to follow him, really. Mustn't make comparisons.'

Dear Frank! Phil was suddenly amused at this display of mingled honesty, generosity and fair-mindedness.

After all, wasn't it for just such qualities that she had married him? She began to feel more hopeful about Jeremy's future. Frank was obviously having second thoughts.

19. Dotty in Court

Mr Jones, the landlord of 'The Two Pheasants', was as good as his word. Soon after six one evening, within a week of Charles Henstock's visit, he rang the bell at the rectory.

Charles opened the door and found himself facing not only the landlord, but also Percy Hodge.

'Come in, gentlemen,' said Charles, leading the way to his study.

'Take a seat, and let me get you some refreshment.'

'Not for me, thanks,' said Mr Jones.

'Nor me,' said Mr Hodge.

The rector's heart sank a little. Had he further antagonized them by calling upon them earlier?

'We've come about the graveyard business,' said Mr Jones, coming straight to the point. 'I promised to turn it over in my mind.'

'Indeed, yes. And what is your decision?'

'I thought I'd have a word with Perce here,' said the landlord, refusing to be hurried.

'Very sensible.'

'And Perce and I had a good sit-down talk about it, didn't we?'

'That we did,' said Percy. 'We fairly thrashed it out.'

'And in the end,' continued Mr Jones, 'we decided that the place is a proper eyesore as it is.'

'Disrespectful too,' added Percy.

They sat back with an air of finality, and the rector's heart sank still further.

'It is indeed,' he agreed. 'That's why we felt something should be done.'

'Yes. We saw that,' said Percy. 'I said to Bill here: "That's a fair eyesore, that graveyard, and something's got to be done about it." Didn't I?'

'You did, Perce.'

'Good,' said the rector faintly. He was beginning to feel slightly dizzy.

'So we came to the conclusion that *provided* our family graves were left alone we'd agree to the levelling and general tidying-up, like you said.'

Charles Henstock gave a great sigh of relief. To his surprise and shame, he felt tears pricking his eyes. He had not realized how deeply he felt about the matter until now.

'My dear Mr Jones, I can't tell you how grateful I am!'

He turned to Percy Hodge.

'And to you too, Mr Hodge. This is a most generous and public-spirited gesture. I shall certainly see that the graves in that corner remain as they are.'

'What about Mrs Cleary's?' asked Percy.

'She is away at the moment,' said Charles, 'but I propose to call on her within the next day or two, as soon as she is back.'

He remembered something suddenly.

'And what about your two men?'

'They're agreeable,' said Percy shortly. The rector decided not to press the matter now, but to have a word in private with Percy's employees later.

Mr Jones stood up.

'Well, sir, I'm glad you're pleased. We didn't want to be awkward, and now we know our people won't be disturbed, we're quite content. I must be off now. I've left the wife in charge of the bar, and we'll be getting busy soon.'

The rector shook hands with his two parishioners, and took them to the door.

The night was still and icy-cold. The wide-spread pall of snow reflected a little light.

'I'll be at church next Sunday,' said Percy gruffly, ramming on his cap.

'I am thankful,' said Charles sincerely, raising a hand in farewell.

Later that evening, the rector crunched across the snow to tell Harold Shoosmith the good news. The moon was rising, a splendid golden full one, glinting on the snow and throwing the dark trees into sharp relief.

'It's a beautiful night,' said Harold in greeting.

'In more ways than one,' agreed Charles, settling by the fire. He told Harold the good news.

'And now I have only Mrs Cleary to see and Martin Brewer who works for her,' went on the rector. 'And I really should have a private word with the Howard brothers. I'm not too sure if they really agree with Percy Hodge. It would be a bad thing if they have been coerced.'

'I don't think there will be much opposition from them, or from Mrs Cleary and young Martin Brewer. I must say, Charles, you have handled the thing very diplomatically.'

'I don't think that I can lay claim to diplomacy, Harold. Let's say that Thrush Green preferred to remain united when it came to it. The very thought of courts and lawyers was enough to bring out the good solid British quality of independence.'

'Talking of courts,' said Harold, 'isn't it tomorrow that Dotty's case is heard? Are you going?'

'Yes, I thought I would stand by her.'

'Unfortunately, I have to go to London to settle some business affairs, otherwise I'd join you. Poor woman! I hope that Justin gets her off.'

'I have every confidence in him,' said the rector firmly. Harold refrained from voicing his own doubts.

'Did I tell you,' said Charles, 'that we have copied your

example and bought a red shade for our sitting-room lamp? It makes such a warm glow.'

'I'm flattered.'

'And Dimity has made a long draught excluder for the bottom of the door. Most efficient.'

'A sausage? Why, we used to have one of those, I remember,' said Harold. 'What a good idea! The rectory tends to be a little draughty, I know,' he said, making the understatement of a life-time.

'Well, it all looks much more snug,' said Charles, 'inspired by this room. I thought credit should be given where credit's due.'

He rose to his feet.

'Must be off. Court starts at ten in the morning, so I want to get ahead with my correspondence. I thought of calling on Dotty tonight, but it may be kinder not to. She may be washing her hair or something,' he added vaguely.

Harold doubted it, but kept silent, and showed his kind-hearted friend out into the black and silver world.

At Lulling Woods, Dotty Harmer leant on her gate and surveyed the peaceful landscape. The air was very still. The full moon, turned from gold to silver in its majestic ascent, lit the snowy scene with a gentle radiance. To Dotty's left, the bulk of Lulling Woods showed navy-blue against the starry sky, with one warm red spot where the wood cutters had made a bonfire that afternoon.

Dotty had watched the blue smoke spiralling aloft in the quiet air. Now only the embers glowed, the aftermath of the two men's energetic work with the axe and electric saw. In that black and white world, it added a touch of colour, of warmth and, Dotty thought, of hope.

A mood of resignation enfolded her. What would be,

would be! She had worried herself into a state of suspended animation, unable to think clearly, or to care very much what the outcome of tomorrow's hearing would be.

She was content now to drink in the tranquillity of the view before her. There was something strangely comforting in being alone with elemental things, the moon, the snow, the distant fire. A mere summons to court seemed ephemeral in their presence. Guilty or not guilty, the moon would rise again tomorrow, the snow would remain, the fire would be rekindled.

Dotty took a deep breath, and realized how bitterly cold she felt. She turned her back upon the scene of her comfort, much fortified, and made her way to bed.

It was clear and bright again next morning when Charles Henstock called for Dotty, as he had arranged to do some days earlier.

'I am going in any case,' he replied, when she demurred, 'and parking is always difficult near the court house. Besides, you will have enough to worry you without the bother of driving.'

And so Dotty entered the rector's car looking surprisingly well-dressed for once. It was true that her stockings were in folds, and that her hair escaped in wisps from underneath a formidable black hat which must once have been her mother's, Charles surmised. But she wore a fur coat, which Charles had never seen before, and her black suede gloves were impeccable.

'Allow me to say how nice you look, Dotty,' said the rector.

'Thank you, Charles. I hope I know what's fitting to the dignity of a court of law. You didn't imagine I'd be in my gardening outfit?'

To tell the truth, Charles would not have been surprised to

find his eccentric friend in just such a garb, but changed the subject.

'Dimity insists that you come back to our house for a meal, whatever the time.'

'That is kind of her. I should love to.'

They drove slowly up Lulling High Street, passing the three Miss Lovelocks in snow boots, scarves and Sunday hats, all making for the same destination.

'Vultures,' said Dotty mildly.

'I beg your pardon?' Charles sounded startled.

'Nothing. I was thinking aloud.'

They entered the market place. The court house flanked one side of the square, an ornate Victorian building comprising various municipal departments as well as the court on the ground floor.

Justin Venables was waiting for his client in the doorway. Charles dropped his passenger, watched the two meet, and then drove round to find a parking place.

The court room, when he entered it, was less than half full. It was Charles's first visit to Lulling Magistrates' Court, and he looked about him with interest.

It was a lofty pseudo-gothic building, with all the woodwork varnished to a sticky brown. Like a treacle-well, thought Charles, who was a devotee of *Alice in Wonderland*.

The public benches were rather uncomfortable, and he wondered if the benches set high on the dais in front for the justices were any more comfortable. If not, he was sincerely sorry for those magistrates who were obliged to spend the day there.

The dock stood on his left, a sturdy structure of carved, well varnished wood and brass, and at the front of the court, on the right, were the jurymen's benches, facing the witness box.

The benches where counsel and solicitors were seated were directly ahead of him, and he could see Justin Venables, silver head bent in conversation with another local solicitor. There were two more people there, one, Charles guessed, the prosecutor for the police. If he were the six-footer with the massive shoulders of a rugby forward, and a jutting jaw, then Charles trembled for Dotty. His appearance alone was enought to strike terror into any heart.

At that moment, the gowned usher stood up at the side of the court and spoke in a tremendous roar.

'The court will be upstanding!'

They all rose obediently, and watched the three magistrates file in, followed by Mr Pearson who went to his desk below the dais and stood facing their worships.

Lady Winter led the way, wearing a grey flannel suit, a blue silk blouse, four rows of pearls and a fur hat.

Mrs Fothergill followed in a dashing brown and white dog-tooth check, a gold brooch and no hat, while Mr Jardine decorous in navy-blue pin stripe stood in front of the large chair in the middle beneath the royal arms.

Polite bows were exchanged. The magistrates, clerk and everyone else took their seats, and proceedings began with the granting of occasional licences to various local publicans, and other everyday business.

It was during this part of the proceedings that the door opened to admit six venerable gentlemen from the neighbouring almshouse. Charles had heard that they enjoyed a morning session at court, and were consequently something of experts on British justice. Certainly, their forecasts of the verdicts found by the bench after long and weighty discussion by that august body were usually the same. If anything, they were inclined to be a little stiffer in their sentences when the victims were elderly, and on the whole disliked probation for anyone over the age of twenty. Some in

Lulling maintained that they would prefer to face the men from the almshouse, who saw things perhaps more clearly than magistrates who had had their brains addled by a lot of case-reading and attending conferences.

The old men settled wheezily into the bench behind Charles, arranging sticks, undoing scarves and having recourse to their handkerchiefs after the cold air outside.

'Started on time for once,' said one to his neighbour.

'I see Pendle's prosecuting. Ought to be done by dinner time. He don't waste words.'

'But Mr Jardine's a rare one for retiring. Wants a drag, I daresay. Proper chain-smoker.'

The usher gave a stern glance towards the whisperers, who subsided slightly.

'Old Tom thinks hisself God Almighty, in that there gown,' muttered one softly, just behind Charles. 'He forgets we can remember him sitting on the kerb with his bottom through his breeches.'

Two youths appeared in the dock flanked by a policeman. They faced charges of stealing from Puddocks', the stationers at the corner of the market square, and of assaulting a policeman in the execution of his duty.

They pleaded guilty, through their solicitor who was sitting beside Justin Venables, and grinned sheepishly at each other when told to sit down.

Mr Jardine, who had served in the army in his youth, always did his best to overcome the natural repugnance he felt for long unwashed hair, dirty blue jeans, and sweat shirts bearing such legends as: 'I am the Greatest', 'I love Everyone' or simply 'Tottenham Hotspurs'. But he drew the line at giggling in court, and chewing gum, in which the present offenders were indulging.

'Take that stuff out of your mouth,' he directed sharply, 'and behave yourselves.'

Meekly, they removed the offending gum, gazing at their fingers in bewilderment.

'Give it 'ere,' said the policeman, producing an envelope. The matter was placed within, and the usher put it ceremoniously in the waste paper basket.

'Your worships,' began the six-foot prosecutor, 'the facts of this case are as follows. At three-twenty on the afternoon of Thursday, December 8th, in answer to a telephone call from the manager, Police Constable Carter proceeded to Puddocks', the stationers, where these two young men had been detained.'

Charles found his attention wandering. He looked discreetly about him. Two young men from the local newspaper were scribbling busily at a side table. Would this case make headlines? No doubt an assault on a policeman would. And quite right too, thought Charles. Policemen had enough dirty work to do without being attacked into the bargain. He began to muse about one of his godsons who was now a police sergeant in Leeds.

A change of voice brought his attention back to the court. The youths' solicitor was now making an impassioned plea for leniency, emphasizing that this was only their second time in court, they had no homes and had been out of work and sleeping rough at the time of the theft and assault. He did the job so well, that Charles would not have been surprised to see tears in the eyes of the justices, but they appeared impervious.

When the solicitor had taken his seat, the chairman conferred briefly with his colleagues.

'The bench will retire to consider this case,' he announced, and stood back for the ladies to precede him into the magistrates' retiring room.

'Court will be upstanding!' shouted the usher, and it was.

'Havin' their coffee now,' said one of the old men. 'They

always retire just after eleven. You going to try a cup out of that new machine?'

'I'm durned if I'm putting a bob into that contraption to get a lousy cardboard cup of wishy-washy chicken soup I don't want, when I'd put me money in for coffee,' said his neighbour stoutly. 'It's a ruddy swindle.'

'He's right,' agreed another.

There was a general relaxation in the courtroom, people moving across to speak to friends, and the solicitors standing up to consult each other. Charles waved to the Misses Lovelock and was embarrassed to receive a blown kiss from Miss Bertha, which he acknowledged with a formal bow.

The clerk, who had gone out later to join the magistrates, now returned, and the court room became rather more seemly. Three minutes later their worships returned.

'You will be remanded in custody for three weeks for reports,' said the chairman. 'We need to know more about you before we pass sentence.'

The youths followed the policeman from the dock.

'Back to the bloody glasshouse,' muttered one, as he passed Charles.

'Told you they was off for coffee,' said the old man behind him. 'They could've done that without retiring, and saved a lot of time.'

'Call Dorothy Amelia Russell Harmer,' said Mr Pearson. The usher departed into the lobby.

'Dorothy Amelia Russell Harmer,' echoed round the building.

Justin Venables stood up awaiting his client. She entered briskly, pointing to the dock.

'Do I go in there?' she enquired of the usher.

'No, no,' said Mr Venables hastily. 'Come and take your place by me.'

Dotty's case had begun.

'You are Dorothy Amelia Russell Harmer of Woodside, Lulling?' asked Mr Pearson.

'I am,' said Dotty politely.

'I appear for Miss Harmer,' said Justin to the bench.

'The charge against you is that on 20 October of last year, you drove a motor vehicle on a road, namely Lulling High Street, without due care and attention, contrary to Section 3 of the Road Traffic Act 1972. How do you plead?'

'Well, naturally – ' began Dotty, looking nettled.

'*Please*,' said Justin hastily. 'My client pleads 'Not Guilty' to the charge.'

'Sit down, please,' said Mr Jardine.

The prosecuting solicitor rose to his full six feet, and gave the facts of the case concisely.

'And I shall be calling three witnesses,' he added. 'The first is P.C. Darwin.'

That officer carried a well-thumbed notebook in case his memory needed refreshing. Hardly surprising, thought Charles, when you heard how long it took to bring a case before the court! He himself would be hard put to it to tell anyone what he had done the day before, let alone four months earlier!

He gave his evidence clearly and agreed with Justin Venables, in cross examination, that Miss Harmer had given every possible assistance after the accident. He then made way for Mr Giles, the second witness.

Mr Giles kept a music shop in Lulling High Street almost opposite Mr Levy's butcher's shop. He was a frail elderly man, white-haired and wearing glasses. He took the oath in a quavering voice.

Yes, he had witnessed the accident, he told the bench. He had heard the crash and said to his assistant –

'You mustn't tell us what you said,' Mr Jardine told him.

'Well, *he* said –'

'Nor what *he* said,' replied Mr Jardine firmly. 'It is hearsay, you see, Mr Giles.'

'No, I don't see,' said the old man, with a flash of temper. 'How am I to tell the truth, the whole truth and nothing but the truth, if you won't let me?'

'As a result of what you heard,' said Mr Pearson, coming to the rescue, 'what did you do?'

Things then proceeded more smoothly.

Justin Venables made a shrewd point by asking about Mr Giles' spectacles. Was he short-sighted or long-sighted?

He was short-sighted.

Was he wearing his spectacles when he saw the accident?

'Probably,' said Mr Giles, now a trifle rattled.

'If you were *not* wearing them you would be unable to see clearly what was happening at a distance of some thirty yards?'

'I could see quite a bit,' said Mr Giles.

'But you can't say positively that you *were* wearing your spectacles.'

'Not on oath, no.'

Mr Venables sat down looking smug.

The third witness was a woman shopper who had been on the pavement at the time of the collision. She answered the prosecutor's questions clearly, but added little to the evidence. Justin did not cross-examine her.

'I will call my client,' he said, when the prosecutor sat down.

Dotty entered the witness box and picked up the New Testament.

'Please remove your glove,' said the usher.

'As you wish,' said Dotty, tugging at the splendid suede pair.

She took the oath firmly.

'Now, Miss Harmer, will you direct your answers to the

bench,' said Justin, 'although I am asking the questions?'

Dotty turned obediently, recognized Mrs Fothergill as an acquaintance, and wished her 'Good morning' affably.

Mrs Fothergill gave a sickly smile, but forbore to reply. Lady Winter and the chairman ignored Dotty's civility, and remained impassive.

'You are Dorothy Amelia Russell Harmer, residing at Woodside, Lulling?' said Justin, in dulcet tones.

'You know I am!' responded Dotty, astonished.

'A formality,' murmured Justin. Good heavens, was she going to be in one of her prickly moods?

He led her, with exquisite caution, through her narrative. It soon became clear that despite her odd appearance and a certain impatience with some of the questions, Dotty was transparently honest about the whole affair. She was not in the least put out by some fairly searching questions by the prosecution, and even congratulated the police in having such a pleasant young fellow as Mr Darwin in the force, before Justin could quell her.

Mr Levy, enjoying every moment of his public appearance, was equally hard to restrain.

'You saw the boy riding before the accident?' asked Justin.

'If you can call it riding,' said Mr Levy. 'He was on a bike far too big for him – sawing away he was, wobbling all whichways, and yelling to his mates. He swerved straight into Miss Harmer. She was well into the middle of the road. I'll take my oath on it –'

'You have,' put in Mr Pearson drily.

'And I've known Miss Harmer since she was a little girl, and she's as straight as a die! She'd say if she'd been at fault. It was that ruddy boy – begging your worships' pardon – as crashed across her path.'

'Miss Harmer's integrity is not in question,' said Justin

austerely. 'Just let us take your account of the boy's movements, point by point.'

With some difficulty he led his ebullient witness through
his story. The prosecutor had no questions to ask. Nor had the
bench.

Justin's last witness was one of the teaching staff who had
been in the playground when the accident occurred. He was
a nervous young man, but Justin soon put him at ease, and he
agreed that the boys were rather noisy and excited when they
left school, and did not take as much care as they should about
traffic conditions. He agreed with Mr Levy that Cyril
Cooke's bicycle was in a poor state and much too big for
him. He himself had told Mrs Cooke so, and suggested that
the boy walked to school. She had not been co-operative.

By now it was almost one o'clock, and Charles was
beginning to get hungry. The almshouse men had shuffled
away some half-hour earlier, but the rest of the spectators
were obviously waiting to hear this case completed.

Justin Venables gave a brief but well-expressed summing
up on behalf of his client, pointing out that she had held a
licence for almost half a century, and that she had no previous
convictions. To his mind, the prosecution had failed to
prove the charge and he suggested, with all due respect, that
it should be dismissed.

'Bench will retire,' growled Mr Jardine, and Mrs Fothergill led out the three.

Charles remained standing to ease his aching back. Who-
ever designed the public seats at Lulling Court deserved to be
sentenced to sitting in them for twenty-four hours non-stop,
he decided.

The Misses Lovelock, aflutter with scarves and gloves,
came up to speak to him.

'Didn't Dotty do splendidly?' quavered Miss Violet.

'Surely she will be found not guilty?' said Miss Bertha.

'I always knew she was a cautious driver,' said Miss Ada. 'I hope that horrid boy gets sent to a penal institution.'

Charles did not feel equal to explaining that the boy was not being charged, only Dotty, and was spared further conversation by the return of the justices.

Dotty remained standing by Justin Venables. Suddenly pale, she looked incredibly old and tired. Charles felt shaken with anxiety for her. What an ordeal! He would be glad to get her into his car and back to the haven of the rectory and Dimity's ministrations.

Mr Jardine cleared his throat with peremptory honkings.

'We find you not guilty of the offence with which you have been charged.'

Dotty looked with bewilderment towards Justin Venables, who was smiling and bowing.

'The case,' explained Mr Jardine, looking directly at Dotty 'is dismissed.'

Dotty inclined her head graciously, and murmured thanks.

'The court will adjourn until two o'clock,' said Mr Jardine.

Everyone stood as the bench retired. The door to the magistrates' room had scarcely closed when Dotty's clear voice was heard.

'Could you, by any chance, lend me a handkerchief, Mr Venables?'

Head up, back like a ramrod, Dotty faced her solicitor. Tears were coursing down her papery old cheeks and splashing unchecked upon the fur coat.

But, through the tears, Dotty's expression was one of utter triumph.

20. Peace Returns

News of the outcome of the court case soon swept Thrush Green and Lulling. Approval was general, although Albert Piggott, and one or two other curmudgeons, expressed the view that it was a pity Dotty would still be able to terrorize the neighbourhood with her driving.

Mrs Cooke, when told of the verdict, executed a complete *volte-face* and said she had told her Cyril, times without number, to give over riding his dad's old bike, and now look where it had led him. She prophesied a piece of his dad's tongue for getting in Miss Harmer's way, and causing everyone a mint of trouble.

Dotty herself, after her brief spell of emotion occasioned by relief, appeared to forget all about the incident, and returned to her many chores in the cottage and garden. It was noticed, however, that the car rarely came out of the garage in the weeks that followed.

The snow was a long time in clearing, but gradually the grass showed again on Thrush Green, and the first early crocuses began to spear the ground.

The rector rang Mrs Cleary, a day or two after Dotty's case, to see if he might call on her to talk about the graveyard. To his amazement, that lady seemed anxious to settle the matter there and then.

'I heard that Mr Hodge and Mr Jones have climbed down,' said the imperious voice at the rector's ear. 'In which case, I think it pointless to continue with my objections.'

The rector rallied from the shock.

'There are one or two points I should like to discuss, nevertheless,' he said. 'We have a sketch map showing our plans for that part of the churchyard where your own family are buried. I should like to show you that.'

'I take it none of my family would be disturbed?'

'None, Mrs Cleary. Simply, their surroundings would be much beautified.'

There was silence for a while.

'Very well. I'm content that you should go ahead, if the others have agreed. I'll vouch for Martin Brewer too.'

Really, thought the rector, anyone would think Lulling were ruled by despotism – one could only hope it was a benevolent one.

'I shall have a word with young Brewer myself,' said Charles firmly.

He broached his second point.

'Would you consider withdrawing your resignation from the parochial church council? I have persuaded Mr Hodge to serve again, now that this little difference has been sorted out, and we should all be glad if you would return to us.'

'I will think about it,' said the lady graciously. She sounded mollified, thought Charles thankfully, as he replaced the receiver.

During the next week he managed to buttonhole the two Howard brothers, as well as Martin Brewer, and was shaken to find how little they really cared about the matter of the churchyard.

'Mr Hodge is boss. We does as he says. We lives in his cottages, see,' explained one of the brothers, as though that made the whole thing completely understandable.

Martin Brewer's attitude was much the same, but tempered with gratitude for Mrs Cleary's generosity in providing a job while he was without a driving licence.

'They don't seem to have any minds of their own,' said Charles despairingly to Dimity.

'They do, dear. But they know which side their bread is buttered.'

The rector still looked pensive.

'Cheer up,' said his wife, 'now you can sit down and apply for the faculty with a clear conscience, and leave it all in the lap of the gods.'

'In the lap of the Chancellor,' amended Charles, smiling at last.

Cyril Cooke was not the only person to suffer from mumps that winter. At the village school the number of sufferers gradually grew from three in January to fourteen in the first week of February.

It meant that work was very much easier, with fewer children in the class, and Miss Fogerty was grateful. The first term of the New Year was always a trial, with bad weather, poor light, and innumerable complaints and epidemics. Added to this general depression was the continuing estrangement from Miss Watson, despite surface civilities.

But one afternoon, when she had seen her depleted class buttoned and shod properly against their homeward journeys through the melting snow, she was surprised to be invited to the school house for a cup of tea.

Miss Watson appeared much agitated as she busied herself with spoons and biscuits, and her hand trembled as she passed Miss Fogerty her cup.

'I hardly know how to begin,' she said. 'Miss Potter has just told me she is leaving at the end of term.'

Miss Fogerty's heart leapt with joy, but she managed to look suitably concerned.

'But why? She seems to have settled down quite well. And heaven knows,' said Miss Fogerty, unable to resist a slight dig, 'she has been given everything she has asked for.'

'I am sorry to say, there is a baby coming,' said Miss Watson. Her face was stern.

'A baby? But she's not married!' cried Miss Fogerty, dropping her spoon.

'It has been known to happen,' pointed out Miss Watson.

'Oh, I know, I know,' agreed Miss Fogerty wisely. 'But how on earth did the silly girl get so involved?'

'She told me, *quite calmly*, that she went away with that young man of hers last summer, and there we are. She was rather nonchalant about the whole thing, which made me cross. She's arranging to marry him in the Easter holidays.'

'What a good thing for the baby,' said Miss Fogerty sincerely.

'But not for *us*,' said Miss Watson with asperity. 'We shall have to be three-in-a-desk all next term, unless we get that dreadful Mrs Spears in as supply, and you know what *that* means!'

Miss Fogerty nodded. Mrs Spears was the only supply teacher in Lulling, a vast noisy creature, reputed to carry a flask of gin among her school books, and much given to teaching the children mid-European folk dances involving a lot of clapping and stamping. The last time she had spent a fortnight at Thrush Green School, she had broken one easel, three tea cups and a child's finger. Miss Watson and Miss Fogerty had suffered from splitting headaches throughout her stay, and had watched her departure with relief.

'You'll put in an advertisement for the post, I suppose?' said Miss Fogerty.

'Oh, I shall see that it goes in immediately, but I don't suppose there's any hope until the girls come out of college in July.'

She replenished Miss Fogerty's cup and sighed.

'Oh, Agnes dear, what a comfort it is to have you to confide in! I can't tell you how I've missed our little chats since Christmas. Nor how *dreadful* I've felt about that bed-jacket! To have upset you so grieved me terribly, as I'm sure you know, Agnes. I hope I'm forgiven. I wouldn't have had it happen for the world.'

Miss Fogerty felt suddenly warm. The vision of a little brook which had remained frozen for weeks near her house but, only this week, had thawed and started to run merrily again, flashed across her mind.

So too did she feel. The ice had melted, the bonds were broken, and joy flowed again.

'It is all forgotten and forgiven long ago,' said Miss Fogerty.

'Ah, Agnes,' sighed Miss Watson. 'Teachers may come and teachers may go, but you and I go on for ever it seems.'

Miss Fogerty decided it was time to change the subject.

'And what about a wedding present?'

'We might club together and buy a cradle,' rejoined Miss Watson, with rare tartness.

Across the green, at Tullivers, one of the mumps' victims sat up in bed.

Jeremy was a woebegone figure, his face and neck so grotesquely swollen that even his mother might have had difficulty in recognizing him if she had met him away from home.

Charles Henstock had called in to see the patient, and to deliver a box of coloured pencils and a drawing book thoughtfully provided by Dimity.

Conversation was limited to expressions of sympathy on Charles's side and sad, inarticulate little cries on Jeremy's. Before long, Charles left the sickroom and accompanied Phil downstairs.

'At least he's in a comfortable bedroom,' said Charles, 'with a kind nurse to look after him. I had mumps at my prep school, and the san. was full, of course. A horrible place – bitterly cold, with lumpy flock mattresses to lie on. And nurse was run off her feet, naturally, and let us know it.'

'Poor Charles!' said Phil. 'I can imagine the misery.'

'The worst thing was being dished out with doorsteps of leathery toast when one could hardly open one's jaws. What is there about boarding schools?'

'I assume that that is a rhetorical question,' said Phil, with a laugh. 'We went to see Frank's the other day, and I was most depressed at the sight.'

'Does Frank still want Jeremy to go away?'

'Let's say he's thinking twice since seeing his old school, but in principle I think he likes the idea of boarding, if only we can find a good place. As you know, I want Jeremy to go with Paul Young in September to Lulling, until he's twelve or thirteen.'

'Well, I'm sure you'll both do the best thing for the boy, as you are at the moment.'

He rose and made for the door.

'Sorry to miss Frank. You know the application for the faculty has gone in? We can only wait and hope now.'

'How soon shall we know?'

'Whenever the Chancellor has time to attend to it. He's a busy man, but very meticulous about his correspondence I know. Maybe within a month.'

'How lovely! And when will the work begin?'

Charles laughed, and held up two crossed fingers.

'Don't go too fast, my dear,' he said.

He had been gone less than ten minutes when Frank arrived home from the office.

'How's Jeremy? Can I go up?'

'Yes, he's awake. Charles has just been to see him.'

She followed her husband up the stairs. Frank, startled at the boy's appearance, stood stock-still in the doorway.

'My goodness! You're twice the boy I left behind me this morning!' he cried.

Jeremy lowered his eyes.

'Not funny,' he muttered.

Frank was instantly contrite.

'You're quite right. It's not funny, and I'm sorry. Got all you want?'

'Yes, thanks,' said the child, looking more cheerful, 'except a drink.'

Phil refilled his glass and sat on the bed watching him take the liquid in painful sips.

Frank surveyed the scene thoughtfully.

'I should have a nap,' advised Phil, at last.

'I think I will,' said the invalid, sliding down the bed. 'My eyes won't stay open.'

Downstairs, Frank turned to Phil.

'He looks pretty snug up there. I had mumps at school. It was ghastly.'

'So did Charles,' said Phil. 'He told me the grisly details of a boarding school illness.'

'I've something extraordinary to tell you,' said Frank, helping himself to a drink. 'About Ribblesworth. Tom had the news this morning at the office.'

'Burnt down?' asked Phil hopefully.

Frank laughed.

'Worse, really. That headmaster's run off – '

'With the matron,' interrupted Phil.

Frank looked at her in astonishment.

'How did you know?'

'She was exactly the sort of person who would be run off with.'

'You must have second sight! That's exactly what's

happened. I never took to that chap. And what a scandal for the school!'

'I daresay it's happened before.'

'Not to Ribblesworth,' said Frank loyally.

He put down his drink and began to pace the room.

'What with going to see it, and remembering mumps at school, and now this business,' said Frank, 'I'm coming round to your way of thinking. Let the boy have a few more years at home as a day boy. Agreed?'

'You know I've never wavered in my feeling on the subject,' said Phil, 'but I think it's downright noble of you to change your mind so generously.'

'Let's go and see the head at Lulling, and get him entered for next September if there's a place, shall we?'

'An excellent idea,' said Jeremy's mother.

Next door, at Doctor Bailey's house, a bridge session had just finished, and Winnie, Dotty, Ella and Dimity sat round the fire with the debris of the tea trolley pushed to one side.

The ladies had discussed their hopes for the faculty being granted.

'Charles thinks of nothing else at the moment,' said Dimity. 'He's like a child waiting for Christmas.'

'Is Albert Piggott going to be in charge when the church-yard is altered?' asked Ella.

'I suppose so,' said Dimity.

'It's a great pity,' announced Dotty, searching in her knicker leg for a handkerchief, 'that my goats weren't al-lowed to keep the place tidy while we were waiting.'

After further scrabbling she produced a crumpled piece of linen and blew her nose with a resounding trumpeting. Only Dotty, thought Winnie, would keep her handkerchief in the leg of her knickers, thus needing to expose wrinkled stockings and bony shanks whenever it was needed.

'Thrush Green's going to see some changes,' said Dimity.

'One is going to happen in this house,' said Winnie, who had managed to keep her domestic plans secret, but now felt that things were advanced far enough to tell her friends. They looked suitably eager.

'Come on, Winnie,' commanded Ella, beginning to roll an untidy cigarette. 'Tell all.'

Winnie explained about the two upstairs rooms, without going too deeply into her own fears at night.

'And Jenny told me yesterday that the old people move next week.'

'How marvellous! And she comes then?'

'No, not for a month or two. There are several things to be done. My nephew Richard is spending a week here soon, putting in cupboards and so on, and the plumber has to fit a sink in the kitchen-to-be. She can stay in her present home for some months if she likes, I gather. Demolition doesn't start until the autumn, so she can take her time.'

'So you'll have someone in the house before long,' said Dotty, remembering that dark afternoon when she and Winnie had exchanged confidences. 'It will be company for you, especially welcome next winter.'

'Lucky Jenny!' exclaimed Dimity.

'Lucky me!' responded Winnie, rising. 'Come upstairs and see what I'm planning to do.'

When Dimity returned to the rectory, she was bubbling over with Winnie's good news and all the plans for Jenny's new flat.

The rector was standing with his back to the small sitting-room fire. In his hand was a letter.

Before she could tell him the news, Charles spoke.

'My dear, I have had a letter from the Bishop.'

'Oh Charles,' cried Dimity, remembering, with sudden

fear, being summoned to her headmistress's study years before. 'What *have* you done?'

'Why, nothing –' began Charles in bewilderment.

'Or is it about the faculty?'

'That is the Chancellor's affair, my dear. This is from the Bishop himself.'

Dimity sat down abruptly.

'Well, tell me quickly. Is there some trouble?'

'Just the opposite. He has been kind enough to make me a Rural Dean.'

Dimity gazed at him open-mouthed.

'A Rural Dean,' she echoed, and then the full glory of the promotion burst upon her, and she leapt to her feet to put her arms round him.

'My darling, how wonderful! And you deserve it too. I'm so glad the Bishop has recognized all your hard work.'

'Others work harder, I expect,' said Charles. 'But I am truly grateful. I must write to him this evening and try to express my appreciation of the honour.'

'Do you know,' said Dimity, sitting down again, 'I feel quite faint. It must be the excitement. The room is swinging about.'

Charles looked alarmed.

'Stay there! I'll find a little brandy.'

'No, no,' protested Dimity, 'I shall soon be all right. I really mustn't start getting a taste for brandy. It's so expensive.'

'Are you sure? Some water then?'

'No, really,' said Dimity, sitting up straight. 'It has passed now. It was simply pure joy! It's heady stuff, isn't it?'

The rector was looking at his letter again.

'It is indeed. Now, Dimity, help me to compose a meet and proper answer to His Lordship for honours joyfully received.'

Later that evening, Charles was in his study, writing a fair copy of his letter to the Bishop, when the telephone rang.

Dimity, by the fire in the sitting-room, wondered at the length of the conversation. Someone in sore trouble again, she supposed. But when Charles entered the room he was smiling.

'That was Bruce Fairfax from the prep school. He has asked me to take Religious Instruction twice a week and I have agreed. He is glad of help and we shall be glad of some extra money.'

Involuntarily, Dimity glanced towards the tall, draughty windows.

'Yes, my dear,' said Charles. 'I think you can safely order some new curtains.'

One blue and white March morning Willie Marchant, one of the postmen at Thrush Green, tacked purposefully up the hill from Lulling, causing alarm to various drivers going about their lawful occasions on the right side of the road.

Willie ignored their shouted protestations, as usual, and dismounted at the rectory. A stub of cigarette exuded pungent fumes, killing temporarily the fragrance wafting from a clump of early narcissi.

He opened the door of the rectory and collected half a dozen letters left there, and put the one he was carrying in their place.

'Only one this morning,' called Dimity, when she went to collect the post. Charles was coming down the stairs.

'But it is the one we've been waiting for,' said the new Rural Dean.

He opened it hastily, and his pink face creased into a beam.

'It's granted!' he said, with a gusty sigh of relief. 'The

precious faculty itself ... to be deposited in the Church Chest. Now, at last after all our battles, we can go ahead!'

On the last day of term, Miss Potter was presented with a set of silver coffee spoons (not a cradle) by Miss Watson and Miss Fogerty, and was given every felicitation for her future happiness.

They were to live in Scarborough, said Miss Potter, and she hoped that they would call if they were ever in that neighbourhood. As the ladies were positive that they would never go so far afield, they were in a position to thank her effusively for the invitation, and Miss Potter departed in a cloud of cordial farewells.

'Well,' said Miss Watson, turning into her classroom, 'I must spend half an hour tidying up here. I suppose you will be going over to your new domain, Agnes?'

'I thought I would take the bulk of my things across,' agreed Miss Fogerty.

'Come back when you've done,' said Miss Watson, 'and have tea with me. I've made a chocolate sponge to celebrate the end of term.'

Miss Fogerty thanked her, and went into her old classroom to collect a large case of infant handwork which was to be transferred to the terrapin across the playground.

The sun was hot on her head as she made her triumphal progress to the promised land. She dumped the case, and stood by the beautiful low window which would do so much to bring on the mustard and cress, the bean seeds and the bulbs, in the happy days ahead.

The little valley leading to Lulling Woods shimmered in the spring sunshine. Somewhere a lark was singing, and in some distant field lambs bleated.

Miss Fogerty sighed with happiness. Here she was – where

she had longed to be. After all the struggles of the winter, peace had come with the spring.

Miss Watson was tapping the school barometer when Miss Fogerty returned. It was a handsome mahogany piece left her by an aged uncle, and as it was too large for the school house it had taken up its abode in her classroom.

'I must say,' said Miss Watson, peering at the instrument, 'it's pleasant to see the needle at "Fair" after "Stormy" and "Rain" and "Change" and all the other unsettled conditions we've had lately. Do you think Thrush Green will remain at "Set Fair" for a time, Agnes?'

'I have no doubt about it,' said little Miss Fogerty.

MORE ABOUT PENGUINS
AND PELICANS

Penguinews, which appears every month, contains details of all the new books issued by Penguins as they are published. It is supplemented by our stocklist which includes around 5,000 titles.

A specimen copy of *Penguinews* will be sent to you free on request. Please write to Dept EP, Penguin Books Ltd, Harmondsworth, Middlesex, for your copy.

In the U.S.A.: For a complete list of books available from Penguins in the United States write to Dept CS, Penguin Books, 625 Madison Avenue, New York, New York 10022.

In Canada: For a complete list of books available from Penguins in Canada write to Penguin Books Canada Ltd, 2801 John Street, Markham, Ontario L3R 1B4.